ISLAND
FIRE

ISLAND FIRE

TOBY NEAL

FOREWORD

'Aumakua

In the Hawaiian cultural tradition, an *'aumakua* is a family god, an ancestor who's been deified through a sacred ceremony. *'Aumakua* act as spiritual guardians and may manifest as an animal, such as a shark, an owl, or a turtle, or as a natural phenomenon, such as a rainbow or a flash of lightning. Knowledge of ancestral *'aumakua*, their particular names, manifestations, and favorite haunts, are passed down through generations. When Hawaiian children are born, they are introduced to their family's *'aumakua,* who will guide and advise them throughout their lives if shown proper respect. If a family's *'aumakua* assumes the form of a shark, that family takes care of all sharks, refusing to hunt or eat them and often leaving offerings of food for them. There are many stories of *'aumakua* intervening to save their descendants from harm, or to chastise them for poor behavior.

Mo'o

Mo'o are ancient Hawaiian dragon deities. Revered as the guardians of freshwater, they were known to inhabit waterfalls, fishponds, and mountain streams. Most mo'o of Hawaiian legend were female and could be helpful protectors or dangerous foes. Mo'o possess supernatural powers; they are able to see things that humans can't, manipulate the seas and rain, and change shape at will. Some of the most powerful mo'o are `aumakua, the deified ancestors of royal Hawaiian families.

—Shannon Wianecki
(Ms. Wianecki writes about Hawaiian
natural history and culture. Find more of her
work at www.shannonwianecki.com)

For Kai and Eva
because you taught me how fun it is to be an aunty

NICK WEBSTER HELD HIS BACKPACK close—everything he owned, packed into two cubic feet of space, a double-sided blue nylon cover belted over it. He looked around the crowded airport waiting area. There was a festive feeling in the air—family groups sharing snacks, a couple of people already wearing leis. He was several hours early for the first leg of his flight to Hawaii, a place Nick had never been.

His new home.

Nick's stomach knotted at the thought. He knew what would take his mind off it—working the room. He would go to an immediate departing gate, dip a crowd close to getting on the plane.

He stood, slinging on the backpack, and drifted with an aimless distracted walk, his gaze apparently on the phone in his hand but really scanning the room. He wore a loose gray hoodie with deep pockets emblazoned with the Notre Dame logo, his ash-blond hair cut short. He looked like a young college athlete, from the tops of his stolen Nikes to the crisp jeans that completed his costume.

Still looking down at the phone, he bumped into a mark standing at the Starbucks stand, doctoring his coffee, and as the man turned with a frown, he raised the hand with the phone in apology. "Sorry, man." The other hand lifted the square bulge of the man's wallet from a back pocket and slid it into the sweatshirt, Nick's turned body concealing the quicksilver movement. Nick never worked a line on its way to the cash register. It was best to dip just after a wallet was used, so the mark took longer to notice it was missing.

Nick drifted on, employing the Drop Coin, Elbow Grab, and Lost Kid's Toy. His heartbeat spiked with excitement—he'd never had such rich, easy pickings in his chosen profession. Even the train station near where he'd lived in Chicago wasn't this good. Everyone's guard was down. They'd bought tickets to Hawaii, they were already on vacation, and they were in a safe place where they'd been "screened."

It was really kind of unfair. But Nick would need everything he could get where he was going, in case he didn't want to stay there.

When the hoodie's pockets were bulging, Nick cycled through the men's room, and in a bathroom stall, he sat on a toilet and skinned the poke off the wallets. No point keeping credit cards—the marks would have canceled them by the time he got anywhere he could use them. He unbelted the cover on his backpack and stowed the IDs of two men roughly matching his own looks that he'd taken the time to work—six foot, in their twenties. He packed the cash into the black money belt circling his narrow hips.

People thought money belts were lame. Actually, they were one of the only places he couldn't get into easily.

Nick stood up, setting the backpack on the back of the toilet, and unzipped the hoodie. On the inside, which became the outside, a bold Chicago Bulls logo gave him a new look. He zipped up the black and red sweatshirt and flipped the nylon cover on the backpack over to the red side. Before he exited, he put the hood up over his head and curved his back into the shape of a sullen teen.

He waited a long moment until the roar of the hand dryer and rustle of other bathroom users ceased. Nick slipped out and dropped ten discarded wallets filled with memento photos, IDs, and credit cards into the steel trash bin. Sheep, his friend Dodger had called the marks. They deserved to be fleeced of what he so easily took.

Bea Whitely knew what to expect by the way her dad's feet sounded on the steps when he came home. She lifted her head, ears tuned like a deer at a watering hole, to listen. The crackling of fish frying in the pan at her hand didn't drown out a beat of extra energy in the tread of his work boots as he climbed to the porch, and she exhaled relief.

Tonight should be a good night.

She glanced at her reflection in the window over the sink—a brown, lanky girl with a long dark braid and shadowed green eyes. Her hair was neat, her tank top and basketball shorts modest—nothing for him to find fault with.

The screen door creaked, and her father came in.

"Hi, Dad. How was your day?" It was what he wanted her to say. Even a variation wasn't a good idea. Bea flipped several small papio in the skillet, all she'd been able to catch casting off the beach.

"Okay." William Whitely pulled a sweat-soaked bandanna off his neck and hung it on the peg on the back of the door. He took off the stained John Deere cap and hooked it over the bandanna. The summery scent of cut grass clung to him, almost masking the underlying tang of sweat and last night's booze. He sat on one of the straight-backed kitchen chairs, loosened his work boots and toed them off. They hit the linoleum floor one at a time.

Thump.

Thump.

"Fish again, Beatitude?"

She'd always hated when he used her full name. Bea was such a better fit.

"Sorry, Dad. We need to go to the grocery store." Groceries on the tiny island of Lanai cost four times the national average because all food and necessities had to be flown or boated in, and there was only one small store serving the island. Bea made it her business to catch something every day to supplement their meager budget.

"Hey, Dad. Come check my work," Sam called from the living room. Bea shot a narrow glance at him—he was trying to distract Dad, prevent an argument. Thirteen-year-old Absalom Kanekoa Whitely had been born with a clubfoot—bent inward and missing two toes. Something about the disability, or Sam himself—Bea had never been able to tell which—made Dad extra hard on him.

4

And still Sam tried to protect her.

William stood up from the chair, a process of unfolding that was as painful to watch as it must have been to perform. He was a tall man with long arms corded from work and big, hard hands. His face was seamed with weather and drink, furrows of deep-etched grief bracketing a mouth like a tight purse. He shambled into the living room, where Sam sat on the floor at their coffee table, homeschooling books spread around him.

"Show me what you've been doing, boy."

William sat on the rump-sprung tweed couch and dragged the notebook over. Sam got up and sat next to him.

"Check my answers." Sam's brown eyes sparkled with pride. He was a slender, wiry boy just beginning the growth spurt that would make him tall. His rumpled brown hair was a little long—Bea would have to clip it soon. He handed his father a pencil. "I got all of today's lesson and some of tomorrow's done."

Bea served up the plates and called them to the table. They ate dinner, and afterward the two of them resumed schoolwork review while Bea cleaned up.

"Taking out the scraps." Bea scooped the trimmings from the dinner prep into a bowl, including one last whole fish no one had eaten. Neither her father nor brother looked up—salt-and-pepper head bent toward brown, their voices soft. Bea slipped out the door onto the porch, slid her feet into rubber slippers, and trotted the scraps out to the chicken coop at the back. She dumped the fish leavings in. The hens, loose during the day, ran out of their roosting spots to peck up the offal. Rainbow, their horse, pushed her head over the sagging barbed-wire fence and nickered. Bea gave her a handful of green bean scraps and a nose rub.

A conflagration of sunset bloomed against approaching dusk, catching her eye. The purpled hump of nearby Molokai Island loomed across the Kolohi Channel to her left, the wide hammered-metal ocean streaked with sunset. The ball of sun was unusually bright, almost pulsating, the sky strobing with colors. Rubbing Rainbow's ears as she gazed at the strange sunset, Bea missed her mother, dead three years now, a pain under her sternum she'd tried to grow used to.

Mama would know what was going on with the sunset. Angel Kanekoa Whitely's Hawaiian roots on Molokai had given her a deep knowledge of the natural world, and she'd passed on all she could to her children.

Bea leaned her forehead on the mare's blazed face, breathing in the comforting horsey smell. "I'll be back for you later, girl."

She had one last pet to feed. She went around the back of the house, which was built on a slope. A slatted storage area marked with a plywood door made the most of the falling-away ground. She heard a soft whuffle from under the house and slipped inside the dim space.

Hi, Beosith, she thought as she squatted and extended her hand, holding the whole fish still wrapped in a paper towel.

Lambent golden eyes emitting light revealed the dragon's location as he opened them. He moved closer with a rustling of scales, a dry sound like something slithering through straw.

Bea. How is he tonight? The *mo'o* dragon's long black tongue snaked out and lifted the fish, paper towel and all, off of her hand and into his mouth. She saw the faint sparks, heard the crunching of the fish's bones as the *mo'o* made short work of it. Hawaiian dragons made water their home, but Beosith could still generate fire.

He seems okay. I have to get back, though.

You know I'm here if you need me.

I know. Sorry there wasn't much to eat tonight.

I can do my own fishing. His blue-purple hide camouflaged him so well in the dim, striped light of the flaming sunset that when the dragon closed his eyes, he vanished.

Sam sat on the overturned wooden box in his room after dinner, the battery-operated reading lamp on the side table casting illumination over the old toaster oven he was working on. Bea swung through the dump on her trips into town to sell fish from the reef, and she'd pick up broken appliances from the rubbish for him to fix with the little soldering set Mama had given him for Christmas the year before she died. Bea resold the ones Sam was able to fix back in Lanai City.

Fixing things. It was what Sam could do. When he was focused on figuring out a problem, he didn't think about missing Mama or worry about pissing Dad off, or even remember how lonely he was, stuck out here at the house without any friends.

Sam touched a tiny bit of solder wire with the iron. It hissed as it ran to the broken wire contact at the back of the toaster oven. The solder seemed to vanish, drawn in to the break in the wire and filling it as if by magic. He lifted the hot iron, and a tiny curl of sulfurous black smoke rose from the tip.

The join looked good. Sam examined the worn cord, and it seemed intact. He plugged the cord into the wall socket. Their electrical system was run off of batteries that stored about a day's worth of electrical juice for every hour they ran the generator, which they did as little as possible since gas had passed seven dollars a gallon on the tiny island.

Sam pushed the lever turning the toaster on and watched with satisfaction as the wires inside glowed to life. They could probably get at least five dollars for it at the little resale shop Papa Obajan ran behind his house.

Sam turned off and unplugged everything. He could hear the rumbling of Dad's snores down the hall. As usual, their father had left the dinner table with a flask of Jack Daniel's and headed for bed. Dad's booze took a lot of the family budget, which was why Sam and Bea worked hard and creatively to keep the generator full of gas and food on the table.

Sam got into bed and pulled out his favorite comic, Batman. But even with his little reading lamp on, he spotted a pattern of flickering color in the night sky outside. Sam turned the lamp off and pushed the old sash window up, pressing his face against the screen to see the rippling ribbons of light better.

Purple and green and hot fuchsia, layers of wavering light spanned the black bowl of the heavens. The colored light dimmed the stars and the rising moon, just like the northern lights he'd read about in the geography section of his homeschool program. Did the northern lights show this far toward the equator? He hadn't thought so, but apparently they did. He thought of calling Bea to show her, but he knew she was going out later and would see the light herself.

Sam pulled the window shut and turned the lamp back on, opening the comic, battered from multiple readings. He liked Batman because the Dark Knight didn't have a natural superpower; he used technology to be a superhero. Looking down at his clubfoot, sore just from walking around that day, Sam wished he could figure out a way to get around better. Walking any major distance hurt his foot and twisted the muscles of his back.

They'd done some initial correcting of his foot when he was a baby, but Dad hadn't allowed the further surgeries that were recommended. "God gave you this foot for a reason," he'd said. "Time will tell what it is. Besides, we can't afford it." Mama's protests had been overridden.

Sam wished he could get the foot fixed. He was pretty sure God didn't have anything to do with it.

2

BEA WAITED IN HER BED until the rumbling snores from her father's room signaled sleep. She got out of bed and padded to the door, peering down the short hall of the plantation-style cottage. Sam's door was closed, but she carefully opened it to peer in at her brother. He was on his back, moonlight falling on outflung arms, relaxation in the boy's posture that was never there on waking. She closed the door and tiptoed along the linoleum to the creaky screen door, slipped through it. On the porch steps, she shook out her worn cowboy boots in case of roaches or centipedes and slid her feet into their cool leather depths.

Bea spotted something in the sky as she headed for the paddock. She tilted her head back and saw a rippling veil of green-to-purple ribbons crisscrossing the heavens.

The patterns seemed to be moving, shimmering; a curtain of glorious color shot through with white sparks like falling stars. She gazed in wonder. These phenomena sure looked like the northern lights, something she'd read about that appeared at the earth's poles.

It's something different. Beosith's bell-like voice rang in her mind. Her `aumakua, or guardian spirit, had appeared to her a week after her mother's death.

She remembered the first time she'd seen him. There'd been a scratching on her window. A blue-purple dragon the size of a small pony was sitting on his haunches outside. He looked at her with lantern-gold eyes. *Hello, Bea,* he'd said without words—a ringing like an echo in her inner ear, his unique way of speaking to her mind.

"What are you doing here? What are you?"

A mo'o dragon. Your `aumakua. I'm here to help you.

She'd awoken the next day a little stronger to deal with her mother's loss. She'd seen the dragon often since, and he'd helped her with advice and warnings. She'd wondered at first if she were going crazy, if experiencing such a creature happened to others, but she'd finally stopped wondering how or why he'd come and was just grateful that he had. Most people seldom got to see their `aumakua—let alone get to know a legendary mo`o, the Hawaiian water dragon.

"Why don't you have a Hawaiian name?" she asked him one day. "Beosith doesn't sound like an `aumakua."

I am descended from some of the great dragons of the past, who flew and breathed fire and ate cattle in places far from here. They gave me my name so they wouldn't be forgotten.

That was the first time he shared pictures with her. The giant dragons of the past were mighty indeed and had been hunted to extinction. Now only the mo`o and their small flying-lizard cousins were left in existence.

What is that in the sky? Bea wondered now. *Do you know?*

Sometimes the dragon answered. This wasn't one of those times.

Rainbow gave a snort of greeting at the sight of her. Bea took the bridle off the peg on the shelter wall and slipped the bit into the horse's mouth. Rainbow chomped, rolling the metal with her tongue, as Bea hooked the headstall over her ears.

"Shh. You know the drill, girl." She led the mare to the gate, unhooked the wire loop at the top, and led the horse out to the stump of an avocado tree. She tossed a felt riding blanket over the mare's back and tightened the straps under her belly.

Bea grabbed a handful of mane and gave a little hop, swinging her leg over Rainbow's hindquarters, and hauled herself into place. She squeezed her thighs, and they moved out of the scrim of trees surrounding the little house and up the rutted red dirt road, rendered black-and-white by moonlight. Bea nudged the mare into a trot as they moved away from the property.

Lanai was a humped pear shape, roughly eighteen miles long by sixteen wide, with a single ridge of mountain that captured rain via towering Cook Pines along its crest. Because of the geography, everything but the topmost mesa where Lanai City was located was on a slope—and other than the stand of trees and great outcropping of rock behind their house, the landscape was wind-scrubbed grass and bushes that had grown up to replace the pineapple that once blanketed the tiny island. Nowadays there was one employer—the Fair Isle Hotel chain, with two locations on the island. All the families that made up the town, including their father, were dependent on it for work.

Bea leaned forward, giving Rainbow a little nudge with her heels, and the mare broke into a canter, heading up the road to Lanai City. The grandiose name had always made her smile, as the entire town consisted of a single open grassy square bordered by small shops and a sprawl of cottages that housed most of the island. The island was privately owned, development clustered in the city except for their house, a rogue outlier built by a foreman in the 1950s who'd had a yen for quiet and a special dispensation from Dole Pineapple.

Bea veered off the road to shortcut the rugged slope along a goat trail. Rainbow knew the way and didn't falter.

She reached the crest of rock just above the tiny town of Lanai City. She slid off Rainbow and tied her to the branch of a scrub guava, ascending to the flat sandstone outcropping on top, still warm from the sun. Anticipation to see her friend Jaden made her breath speed up even more than the exertion of climbing.

"Hey." A shadow rose on the opposite side of the rock. Bea's heartbeat picked up.

She and Jaden had been best friends since elementary school, when the Whitely family had moved to Lanai from Molokai so her father could work at the Lanai Lodge as one of the head groundskeepers, a good job that had eroded with time and drink.

Jaden had never minded that she was a girl. He'd cared only that they liked the same things—fishing, diving, riding, and hunting. After Mama died and Dad had pulled them out of school and life in town, Jaden had been the only friend who never gave up on her. He'd been the one to set up their rendezvous spot and get her out fishing and reef picking to supplement the family income.

"Hey, yourself." Bea sandwiched her hands behind her head on the warm rock, looking up at the colorful night sky.

Jaden pointed at the sky. "What the hell's going on up there?"

"Don't swear," Bea said automatically. Swearing was the kind of thing that could slip out in front of Dad. "I've seen pictures of the northern lights. It kind of looks like that."

Jaden stretched out beside her and imitated her posture. He was a lean shadow beside her, but she knew his hard angles and wiry strength, the warm brown of his skin, just as well as her own. She could feel his warmth mere inches away, bringing a tingle along her body that raised the hairs on her arms.

"It's pretty, whatever it is." Silence fell over them as they watched the changing light show above.

"Well, we should probably get down to the reef," Bea said. "It's getting late."

"Sounds good." Jaden grinned, a flash of white in the dark. "Got my weapons." He tapped a mesh bag at his side. It rattled with something metal.

"Mine are at the beach." Bea scrambled back down the rock and untied Rainbow. She mounted and reached out to give Jaden a hand, but, taller than she, he boosted himself up, swinging in behind her to reach around her waist with his arms. Bea stifled the thrill that zipped up her back at his touch—they'd ridden double hundreds of times, she told herself.

The mare set off, heading downhill this time. They made short work of getting to the long, wide-open beach known as Shipwreck Beach because of the giant rusting hulk of an old freighter embedded in the barrier reef.

"I should check the news when I get back," Jaden said. "Maybe there will be something on about the northern lights."

"I hope so."

"It would be great if I could call or text you."

"You know how it is. We don't have a phone—or TV or Internet. Anyway, we can meet again tomorrow night, and you can tell me then. I might hear something on the radio."

The little boombox in the living room was the only link Bea and Sam had to the outside world, and even that was dependent on running the generator. Their father kept their only phone, a minutes-only burner, plugged into a charger locked in his truck.

The tide was out—Bea had checked—and conditions were good for picking opihi, the single-shelled local delicacy that thrived on the rocks of the reef. Catching them always reminded her of happy hours learning reef skills from her mother.

They left the mare tied near a clump of grass. Bea took her shortened three-pronged spear, tabis—sock-like rubberized shoes with a felt sole used to protect feet on the reef—mesh bag, and opihi knife out of a hiding place under a driftwood log. "I should bring my throw net down," Jaden said, not for the first time.

"Yeah, but then you have to rinse it off, and it's heavy."

"I know—but we could get so many more fish at once." Jaden was very good with the circular net cast by hand over schools of fish.

"This is okay. If we had some fresh water down here, it might be worth it, but if you leave the net salty, it'll be junk in a month." Bea slid her feet out of her cowboy boots and into the rubber tabis. "Tide looks extra low tonight."

"Yeah, we hardly need the flashlight with the light show going off in the sky." Jaden had worn his tabis to meet her, and now they walked out onto the reef, picking their way around deeper pools. Jaden pointed a flashlight around the edges of the tide pools where the opihi liked to cling. They worked their way, filling their bags with the circular limpets, to the outer edge of the reef. A line of surf, glowing in the unearthly light, defined the edge of deeper water.

Bea cocked the three-prong spear, stretching the loop of rubber tubing and twisting it halfway down around the aluminum shaft of the spear. It took effort to hold the simple weapon at the ready, but her hands were strong from hours of hard work. She moved away from the beam of Jaden's light, close to a big, deep hole in the reef. She squatted down slowly, watching the shadows moving in the dark water until one swam close to the edge of the pool. She stood and shot the spear in one lightning move.

The spear flew forward into the shadowy water, and she followed it, pushing the spear forward until it hit the bottom. She'd kept the rubber loop that propelled it over her wrist, and now she yanked it back and lifted the spear with a scooping motion so that whatever she'd hit couldn't wiggle off the prongs.

Jaden must have heard the splashing. He shone the flashlight on a fat *aweoʻweo* impaled on the tines. "Nice one."

"There are more in here. These guys like to come out at night. Maybe you should have brought that net."

"Next time. We'll still have extra-low tide tomorrow night." Jaden aimed the light as Bea worked the flapping red fish down the prongs and stuffed it into her bag, already heavy with opihi.

Bea was wading forward slowly, thigh-deep in the inky water of a big tide pool, when she heard Beosith.

Watch out.

She stopped. Lifted the spear high, scanning the water. The dancing light overhead played across the surface, winking and teasing—but darker than the deepest shadow, almost hidden by the distracting glimmer of far-off light, she spotted a sinuous shape.

"Hey!" Nick heard a loud shout from the direction of where he'd been lifting wallets. Nick's heart thundered. His hood was turned up, he was now back to Notre Dame on the outside, and his ears were plugged with earbuds that weren't turned on. His jeans were belted low around his buttocks so they hung in a sullen pile over the expensive Nikes.

He kept his head down, his mind scurrying to recall how he might have "kissed the dog," or let his face be noticed. It was hours later, and he'd stopped working a while ago, getting a little distance and napping while he waited for the flight.

Now in line, he shuffled forward, hoodie low over his face, handing his boarding pass to the gate attendant.

"Hey! Stop that kid!"

Nick didn't react, just slumped in teenager mode down the metal tunnel of the on-ramp leading to the plane. Even as he scanned for his seat on board, he knew he probably wasn't in the clear; even in the air he wouldn't be. They could radio the destination, have him picked up when he got off, or he could get grabbed now.

Being cool was key. At this point he didn't even know if it was him they'd been yelling for.

Nick found his seat, way in the back near the bathrooms. He was on the window, and he quickly stowed the backpack under the seat in front of him, slid out into the aisle and into the tiny bathroom.

He rammed the bolt shut and splashed water on his face, shaking with adrenaline. He'd stay in here until they shut the cabin for takeoff and made him get back in his seat. Hopefully, he'd have shaken the tail by then.

It occurred to him that he spent a lot of time in restrooms and that he'd never liked them. Maybe in Hawaii he'd give up the game and go straight. He'd just have to wait and see what life with his grandparents was like.

3

BEA AIMED AS BEST SHE could and shot the spear, following the three-prong into the water to drive it deep. The black water seemed to erupt around her, and she felt a powerful lashing against her legs and arms. The spear bucked and surged in her hands as she struggled to pin whatever it was to the bottom. She lifted her head and sucked some air, hearing Jaden yelling. The flashlight bounced a yellow lance of light through the water as he jumped in next to her.

"I've got it pinned." She coughed, keeping pressure on the spear and working her arms back up the shaft so she could stand upright. Jaden shone the light down into the water.

A massive moray eel, its head buried in the sandy bottom and pinned down by the spear, wound and rewound its muscular, brown-spotted body around the spear, flailing and lashing the water.

"Damn!" Jaden exclaimed. "That mother's huge!"

Bea moved farther back as the eel's body slithered across her legs. "He'll get off the spear as soon as I lift the prongs off the bottom."

"I'll cut his head off right there." Jaden took his dive knife out of his bag. "Hold the light for me."

Before she could protest, he handed her the flashlight, huffed a few giant breaths to fill his lungs, and plunged underwater.

She shone the light with one hand and put all her weight on the spear with the other, resisting the powerful force of the eel's thrashings. The tableau before her had a nightmarish quality as the flashlight played across bubbles rising from Jaden's waving crop of black hair, his muscular back, and the silver flash of his blade. Poufs of blood that looked black in the water swirled as her friend struggled with the eel. Its frenzied lashing stirred up the bottom, and between the clouds of blood and sand, Bea couldn't see a thing.

Suddenly Jaden burst up out of the water, gasping. Thick as Sam's thigh, the headless eel, still lashing, pumped blood over his hands. She could see it took all he had to keep a grip on it, even without its head.

"Awesome!" He heaved himself out of the pool and ran across the reef for the beach, still wrestling with the writhing corpse.

Bea made the familiar scooping motion with the spear and brought it up out of the water. The three prongs had penetrated the eel just behind its head. Jaws the size of tongs snapped open and shut over teeth like a double row of horse-sized hypodermic needles, and its tiny baleful black eye glared hate at her. Blood ran from the ragged hack job—what was left of its neck—down the shaft of her spear.

She drove the spear back into the sandy bottom and stepped on the eel's head, yanking out the prongs and leaving the head for the crabs.

Bea found herself shaking with adrenaline aftermath as she hauled herself out of the pool and made her way to the beach, where she could still hear an occasional whoop from Jaden. By the time she made her way to the shore, he'd gutted the eel and cut it into several large chunks.

"Might as well go home," he said, holding up a hefty piece. "We've got plenty here."

"Sounds good. Let's clean the rest of these fish."

Thank God her father left so early in the morning—he wouldn't know how late she'd end up sleeping after the nighttime reef raid. Bea made short work of gutting the fish, giving Jaden half. He'd meticulously divided the opihi and eel between the two of them.

"Do you want to keep these, or have me take them to the store?" Jaden knew everyone in town and would sell all the opihi and fish they could spare to the market or restaurants.

"We'll take a little home to eat but we need to sell the rest. We need some more gas for the generator—the hotel cut Dad's hours starting next week, and he doesn't realize how much I have to run the generator just for a few hours of light at night." Bea rubbed sand on her hands and swished them through the salt water to get the fish guts off.

"Okay. I'll bring a full can of gas tomorrow night. Why'd they cut his hours?" Unspoken between them was the fact that Jaden's father had replaced Will Whitely as head groundskeeper at the Lanai Lodge and probably had something to do with that decision.

"He's been drinking during the day." Bea packed her gear with irritable movements. "It's been getting worse."

"I'm sorry."

"It's not your fault. Your dad has to do what he has to do. I'm just bummed Dad's going to be around the house more. I worry about Sam. Dad takes things out on him." Bea hid her gear under the log. She'd never talked about her dad's drinking before. It felt good to acknowledge what a problem it was becoming. "I can't protect him all the time Dad's around."

"I wish there were something I could do. Sam could hang out at our house in town. My brother Jeremy likes him." Jaden swished water on himself to get the worst of the blood from the eel off.

"Dad won't let him go. There isn't anything you can do. But thanks."

They woke up the tired, grumpy mare. The ride back up the trail had a surreal quality to it—the combination of exhaustion, their wetness, and the powerful smells of fish, boy, and horse combined with the kaleidoscope of colors in the sky to make Bea feel disembodied. The light phenomena were now so bright they eclipsed the moon. She shivered, her fingers numb on the reins, and Jaden clasped her close in a hug from behind.

"You're cold."

"Wet clothes. Yeah."

He rubbed her arms briskly. "Let's hurry."

"She's tired." Still, Bea nudged Rainbow into a weary trot. The now-heavy bags bounced against the mare's sides, and the horse snorted, her distaste evident.

"The lights seem to be moving," Jaden commented as he slid off the mare at the jutting rock, their rendezvous point. Bea tilted her head back to see, and indeed the phenomena seemed to have moved a little north.

"I don't know. Maybe it's the earth's rotation? I'll look it up on the computer at home." She had an old PC with *Encyclopedia Britannica* on CD, a poor substitute for Google.

"I'll see what I can find out. See you tomorrow night." He squeezed her dangling calf, a friendly gesture that sent a ripple of feeling up Bea's leg.

She wished these little electric shocks would stop—she felt them changing her friendship with Jaden in some way she wasn't willing to think about—but at the same time they felt good. He took down his bulging net bag, leaving her much lighter one filled with fish and eel chunks.

"Bye." She moved out as Jaden disappeared down the slope toward the town. Bea gave the mare an extra scoop of expensive grain in her bucket back at the house and slipped inside.

Nothing had changed in the hours she'd been gone—snores still reverberated from her dad's room, and Sam's door was still closed. She went into the bathroom and tucked a towel into the crack under the door to muffle the noise as she turned on the shower, stripping out of her soaked clothes and taking them into the galvanized metal surround with her. Under the fall of sun-warmed water they collected through a catchment system on the roof, she rinsed her clothing. Laundry was a bimonthly chore in town she preferred to put off as long as possible.

Bea noticed some reef scrapes on her calves she hadn't felt at the time, and there was a blister in the web of her right hand from holding the rubber loop cocked back on the spear. It didn't matter. Tonight's haul was well worth a few blisters and scrapes.

She washed her long brown hair. Her mother's Hawaiian heritage was most evident in the thick, luxurious carpet of hair, which her father refused to let her cut. Bea's green eyes were the result of William's blue crossed with her mother's brown.

She still remembered her mother, Angel, so well—the humor she'd used to handle William's moods, the affection and hugs she'd lavished on the kids. "I love being Angel Whitely," she'd say. "I can polish my halo all over town."

Her mother had failed to wake up one morning three years ago. An embolism, the doctors said. "Unforeseeable. A fluke."

Bea had tried and tried to wake her mother. Nothing had worked, even her attempts at CPR. She wished she could forget how it felt to try to blow life into her mother's rubbery, cold lips, but the memory could still bring a wave of nausea and grief so paralyzing it bowed her over under the flow of warm water.

When Bea thought of Mama, she felt tightness in her chest like a wall of tears—as if she'd start crying and never be able to stop. She knew Mama would have been sad to see what had happened to them without her. Bea's aunt, Hilary Kanekoa, had tried repeatedly to have the kids come to Molokai to live on the family's ranch as William's drinking got worse, but this year he'd even put a stop to their annual summer visits to Molokai.

Bea still heard him weeping at night. Maybe he just couldn't handle being without them as well as Mama.

Bea turned off the shower, frowning as she toweled off and noticed that her breasts were still growing. She was definitely going to have to get a bigger bra, a situation as challenging as her period starting six months ago—a monthly problem involving mess and secrecy. At almost sixteen, she was a late bloomer, but the changes in her body seemed to make her dad even more paranoid. Asking him for a larger bra would definitely lead to a lecture about staying pure like the Bible said, as if her breasts had a sinful mind of their own. As if she even saw any boys but Jaden.

And where would she get a bra, on Lanai, where there were no real clothing stores? All the other families took their kids on the ferry to Maui, the main island, to shop at Walmart or Sears, but her father hadn't taken them to Maui since their mother died.

"I'll just make it work," she muttered, pulling on another tank top and a pair of loose pajama pants. Maybe Jaden's mom could get her one—but how embarrassing to have to ask. She and Sam had a steady stream of hand-me-down clothes Jaden passed on from his big family, which included two sisters.

Bea hung a dark sheet over the window of her small bedroom so she could sleep in and draped her long, damp hair over the pillow and off the end of the bed. Hopefully, it would dry by tomorrow.

4

SAM AWOKE AS SOON AS he heard Dad rustling in the other room. He tossed his quilt aside and limped into the kitchen, hoisting up loose pajama bottoms. He swung the basket open on the coffeemaker, took out the old grounds and filter and put them in the sealed can on the sink for garden mulch. He had a fresh pot of coffee brewing and was checking out the bag of eel chunks in the fridge when Dad came in—shuffling forward with the gait that said he was tired but the hangover wasn't too bad.

Sam closed the fridge door with a couple of eggs from their chickens in his hand. "Hey, Dad."

"Hi, son." Dad ruffled his hair, heading for the coffee mugs hung in a row over the sink. "Making me breakfast?"

"Yeah." Sam took down the black iron skillet from its hook. "Want some fish? Bea caught some yesterday."

"Sure. Girl's making up for sleeping in."

Sam bit his tongue on defending his sister. He could tell she must have been out very late, and now, at five a.m., the sun was barely staining the sky outside the window with

29

morning pink. He took out a chunk of eel, rinsed it, and cut it into a couple of filets, setting them to cook alongside the eggs. Dad filled his mug with black coffee and headed outside to sit on the steps and wake up, his morning ritual.

Sam sprinkled the filets—smelling delicious—with Lawry's All Purpose Seasoning, one of their indulgences from the Lanai Market. He flipped the eggs just so, but broke one of the yolks. He felt his stomach clench.

Dad came back in as Sam slid the eggs and eel filets onto the plate beside the stove.

"Broke the yolk," he said.

"Sorry, Dad." Sam braced himself but too late—the blow caught him on the side of the head, and he staggered sideways. His bad foot crumpled, and he almost fell, catching himself by grabbing the sink, hanging there awkwardly and hauling himself up.

"Get it right. Thought your mother taught you how." His father stood over him. Sam could hear him breathing, a low snorting through his nostrils like a bull about to charge. Sam held perfectly still, his ears ringing and vision blurry, waiting to see if there would be more. "If you got it right, I wouldn't get mad like this. Now you've made me mad."

"I'm sorry, Dad," Sam whispered. Shut his eyes. Braced himself with one hand on the sink. But the blow came from the other direction this time, and he flew the opposite way. His head caught on the handle of the still-hot frying pan as he went down. It followed him with a clatter, and the heated metal connected with Sam's arm as he hit the floor, wrenching a cry out of him as he landed.

"Leave him alone!" Bea's shout sounded muffled to Sam from the other side of the room as he cradled his burned arm. "Stop it!"

His father picked up the breakfast plate, moved away with it to the back door. "Don't sass me, girl, or I'll give you some, too."

The screen door slammed as Will Whitely went out onto the back porch with his breakfast.

Bea murmured something as she knelt beside Sam, pulling him up, checking him over. His head was ringing too much to decipher the words. He kept his eyes shut, feeling those weak tears he could never seem to control squeeze out from under his eyelids. She hugged him and hauled him up to the sink, turning on the water and letting it run over the burn, and still he kept his eyes shut and felt the tears running. He held his breath so as not to make any noises.

Noises just made Dad madder.

He missed Mama with an ache that really never went away. The way Dad had been getting mean, keeping them home all the time and away from other people, made him want to run away. Like he could run anywhere, on an island as small as Lanai—and with his bad leg.

Mrs. Apucan, Jaden's mother, had asked him one time why he'd never had surgery to fix his foot. He didn't really know how to answer her, and had ended up shrugging and silent.

"Stop it, Bea," Sam finally said, as Bea wiped his face with a wet cloth and put ice in the cloth to cover the burn. He worried one day his eardrum would pop. He wished Dad would hit him somewhere else—like his back or his arms. "I have to fix his lunch."

Lunch was Sam's job. Things had a certain order that had to be followed. He pushed his sister away and limped over to the fridge. His knees were still a little wobbly, but the cool air of the fridge on his throbbing face felt good. He took out a homemade Spam musubi—rice and fried Spam wrapped in nori, pounded black seaweed—a mango, and some cold leftover fish from dinner. He put the food in Dad's lunch box. Bea helped, pouring the rest of the coffee into a thermos.

Dad came back in. He'd put his work boots on and had finished his breakfast, and he put the plate in the sink. He addressed Bea like nothing had happened.

"Get the seeds in from the garden and set them up to dry properly today. I'll be checking both of your schoolwork tonight."

Bea folded her arms and glared at Dad without answering. Sam hurried to set the metal lunch box and thermos on the corner of the table.

"Okay, Dad," he said. "Have a good day at work." It was what their mother had said to Dad every day when he left. It was what he wanted to hear, and Sam said it with feeling. He really did hope his dad had a good day at work.

"Be good." Dad picked up the lunch box and thermos. He walked out onto the porch, and the screen door slammed behind him.

The coast was almost clear—Dad would be gone for another eight hours. Bea wiped down the table, and Sam washed Dad's plate, listening for the sound of the truck's engine firing up, the grumble of it pulling away. Sam didn't relax until it faded into the distance.

Bea had filled a couple of ziplock bags with ice, and she brought them to Sam as he turned away from the sink. "Put these on your face and on that burn."

He took the ice. "Okay."

"I'm going back to bed—Jaden and I worked hard last night." She stomped away, like she was mad at him. Maybe she was. He never seemed able to get things right.

Sam took the ice and his favorite comic and went to his bedroom. He wished he had a friend to read with—but no one ever came to their house, and Sam couldn't walk to town. He put one ice bag on the burn and one on the cheek and eye he could feel getting puffy.

He opened his comic. Batman would never put up with getting hit. Dark feelings choked Sam that he couldn't swallow and he couldn't speak.

5

NICK WAS BACK ON THE plane after a stop in Scottsdale, Arizona, where they let the passengers off to stretch their legs while the plane refueled. He'd been tempted to work an area around a gate headed for Chicago, but the stress of the previous scare had him lying low.

Nick stowed his backpack under the seat, setting his feet on his worldly possessions. A chatty-looking older woman took the seat beside him, and Nick pulled his hood deeper over his face and turned on his earbuds to tune her out in case she tried to talk to him. Cocooned in his self-made cave, eyes shut, he let himself think about what was going on.

His grandparents had retired to Maui, and he hadn't seen them since he was little. He hardly remembered them. His mom had been in college when she got pregnant with Nick, and she'd insisted on keeping him against their wishes. His dad was a fling and had never been part of their lives. Mom had dropped out of college and worked as a waitress, going to school on the side. She'd worked hard to become a nurse, only to die two years ago on an icy road when Nick was fourteen.

His throat worked, thinking about it. He still raged inside at how wrong it was that she was gone—his hardworking, loving mom. They'd never had much, but he'd been on the narrow then. He'd wanted to make her proud.

After she died, Nick had gone into foster care. In foster he'd met Dodger, a kid with fast hands and smooth moves who'd taught Nick a way to take control of his destiny.

He and Dodger had worked together as a team, but Nick would never forget the manacle-like grip of the undercover cop he'd tried to dip closing around his wrist and his last glimpse of Dodger's worried face before his friend melted into the crowd.

At the station, his grandparents had been tracked down and contacted, given a chance to take him or he'd be put away in juvie until he was eighteen.

They'd agreed to take him rather than see their only remaining flesh and blood locked up. Nick guessed they'd felt guilty about not taking him in the first place, though that wasn't what he saw in his grandfather's stern face in the Skype interview with Child Welfare Services.

"This is your chance to get back on the right path, Nick," his grandfather had rumbled, snowy brows pulled together over deep-set blue eyes he recognized as his own.

"We can't wait to see you, honey," his grandma said, reaching out a hand as if she could touch him through the computer screen. "You should have come here right away, but we—we had a hard time after Amanda died."

They had a hard time. Like he hadn't. He didn't think they really wanted him; they were just embarrassed to turn him away in front of Social Services. Nick gritted his teeth. He moved his hands to feel the thickness of the money belt around his waist.

Every time he dipped, he got a thrill that made him feel good, like anything was possible. Unfortunately, the thrill didn't last long, but anything *was* possible with enough money. If he didn't like it at the grandparents', he could take his stolen IDs and go somewhere else. Maybe find Dodger, move out to California. Find his dad, even—a scary idea he'd toyed with over the years. In the meantime, by working the airport he was set up nicely for whatever Maui had in store.

Still holding the money belt, he finally relaxed enough to fall asleep.

Someone was pounding on her door. Bea sat up and threw aside the quilt her mother had sewn years ago from old jeans backed by a flannel sheet, worn soft by washings.

"What?" Bea called, pushing frizzing hair out of her eyes. At least it had finally dried. She'd had trouble falling back asleep after the all-too-familiar scene in the kitchen. She'd been so angry with Dad, and as usual, there was nowhere to go with those feelings.

Sam opened the door, putting his head in. One side of his face was red and puffy, the eye swelling with purple. "Bea, it's almost lunchtime."

"Oh, thanks." Bea swung her legs out of bed. "That's some shiner you've got. Did you put ice on it?"

She knew her voice came out hard, but she couldn't seem to help it. Sam's injury made her mad at Dad all over again. Sometimes it seemed like Sam thought it was *him* she was mad at.

"Yeah. Just wanted to wake you so we can get our schoolwork done. Dad said he wants to see it."

"Yeah. He'll check it. He always does." In addition to all the chores to keep the household running, Bea and Sam had a fairly rigorous homeschool curriculum to get through.

"I made some breakfast for you," Sam said. Bea smelled eggs cooking and something with a fishy tang. "That eel must've been huge."

"Yeah, last night was crazy." Bea bundled her hair into a knot at the back of her head as she followed her brother into the kitchen. She recounted how she'd pinned the eel and Jaden had hacked its head off underwater. Sam had done her eggs just like she liked, over hard with some leftover rice and a slab of eel cooked with garlic and margarine, all of it filling the pan. "Oh my God, I'm so hungry."

She went over and hugged Sam with one arm as she looked into the frying pan full of delicious food, the same frying pan that had left a red burn on her brother's thin brown arm.

All her regrets and fears about Dad rose up to choke her in an inarticulate wave. Dad smacked her sometimes, but nothing like what he did to Sam. She'd never understand it, and somehow she had to make it stop.

Beosith, she thought, her eyes closing as she squeezed her little brother tightly. *Help us!*

It was the first time she'd reached out to her `aumakua that way. But things were only getting worse with Dad. The abuse just had to stop.

I'll try. The *mo'o* dragon sent a warm feeling of reassurance to her, and she clung to it. She had a feeling he'd just been waiting for her to ask for help.

"I'm hungry, too." Sam served them, and Bea carried their plates to the table. She lifted her head in alarm to look at Sam. "Did Dad ask about the eel? Where it came from?"

"No. He knows you go fishing."

Bea took a bite of the eel. The meat was pure white, surprisingly light and springy with a texture like lobster. "This is so good."

"Thanks. It's awesome how you guys keep getting us food. And money." Sam stirred his eggs with his fork, his eyes downcast. "Wish I could come with you."

"Maybe another time. There's only room on Rainbow for two. I also want you to keep an eye on Dad, keep him distracted if he wakes up. I mean, he'd have a hemorrhage if he caught me outside the house at night—not to mention with a boy."

"I know." They each had their job to do. "I got that toaster oven fixed. You can take it into town on your next run."

Bea finished the last of the food, her tummy settling into happy contentment. "Thanks, Sam. Let's do the gardening after we get schoolwork done, and then we can go down for a swim and cool off."

"Okay." Sam carried his plate to the sink, moving with that dragging limp from his bad foot. Bea felt familiar anger looking at his bent dark head as he washed the dishes—Sam never complained, but his disability was unfair and should have been fixed.

Bea took their books down off the shelf and cleared away the last of the meal so they could do their schoolwork at the table. She took out the dog-eared teacher's guide, which adults were supposed to use to coach the lessons, but other than choosing a highly rated curriculum and paying top dollar for it, their father hadn't once looked at the guide.

Today they were doing a lesson on Latin roots in science and their connections to the romance languages. They had the same lesson in a tenth-grade and seventh-grade version. She wondered if the public school kids had Latin and decided she'd ask Jaden tonight.

Jaden was her lifeline to the outside world, just as she was Sam's.

Bea remembered the strange light phenomena and wondered if Jaden had learned anything. She turned on the radio to the news channel—nothing but static. She rotated the dial through all the stations, but still nothing came in.

After several hours of schoolwork they went outside and worked in the garden—a big rectangular plot in full sun. They both wore bathing suits to keep their clothes clean.

Bea had made it her goal not to purchase anything for the garden, an exercise driven by necessity. She kept a well-stocked compost pile, leaves and organic matter, including chicken and horse manure, as the main nutritional elements. Today she harvested seeds. In every crop of green beans, lettuce, tomatoes, bell peppers, or squash, she'd let a few plants go completely to seed, setting the pods or flowers aside to dry and mature for a few months before she replanted them again. It took time and planning, but this was one of her favorite stages. Sam weeded as she moved among the dying string bean plants, harvesting dried pods.

"Taking these to the cave," she told Sam. Her brother was withdrawn and grumpy. His eye had gone puffy and purple, obviously painful. He nodded, and she carried the handfuls of bean pods to their cache—a cave hidden in the outcrop of rock behind the house. She'd set up something of a storeroom in the cool, dry space—shelves of canned food, bedding, gallon jugs of water.

Ever since their mother died, Will Whitely worried that "something bad" would happen. He'd made sure there was a month's supply of everything the house needed out in the cave, "in case of a hurricane." But Bea knew he feared something more than that—other people, losing his job. The cave was the ideal place for storing what they'd collected in case it did. Hidden by a large lantana bush, the narrow slit opening into it was nearly invisible.

Once inside, Bea turned on the light, a dangling bulb their father had rigged up to run off the house's electrical system. The yellow, swinging light illuminated the shelves she'd set up along the wall. She used old coffee cans for storage for the seeds, piercing them with a few holes so air could circulate but keeping rats and other pests out.

She made short work of hulling the beans and set them on a piece of paper sacking inside a coffee can turned on its side. Even though Dad drank a lot of Folgers, she never had enough coffee cans. She checked her other seeds, in various stages of undisturbed drying.

She walked back out. "Let's put in a new vegetable bed. Get some more beans going."

"Why?" Sam pushed sweaty brown hair out of his eyes, still on his knees among the lettuces. His bruised face made her chest tighten. "Do it yourself. You're always telling me, 'Do this; do that, Sam.' You're not my dad. Or my mother." He punched the trowel into the soil with a stabbing motion.

The hurt of his words bloomed into a cramp in Bea's stomach. "Fine. Whatever."

She got out the shovel and hoe and began the unpleasant process of chipping a new vegetable bed into the hard red soil. After a half hour of battling the packed-clay soil, she tossed down the shovel.

"It's getting hot. Let's go down to the ocean and cool off."

"Yes!" Sam got up and dusted off his hands and knees.

"I'm ready, too." Bea cast a glance at the sky, bright with afternoon sun. For the first time she noticed a scrim of phosphorescent sparkles overhead, where she'd seen the northern lights last night. She frowned—she still hadn't found anything out about the lights. It was so bright she put on her old pair of sunglasses before she slipped the bridle onto Rainbow's head. "Let's go down to the big swimming hole."

She and Sam rode double and let the mare walk at her own pace down the path to Keomoku Beach, a long expanse that faced the vast golden island of Maui. The beach was downwind of the bigger island, so it caught all of its floating debris, and they rode past piles of driftwood and ocean-battered trash to a deep, sand-bottomed swimming area.

The sunlight had gone funny, a glaring whiteness to it, and Bea frowned up at the sky through her sunglasses—she could see the flickering bands of color even with them on.

At the swimming hole they slid off the mare and tied her reins loosely to a sturdy bush. It was hot, and Bea bundled her hair on top of her head and pierced it with a stick as she followed Sam.

Sam tore his shirt off, tossing it on the beach, and ran into the water. His moment of grumpiness seemed forgotten as he turned to splash her.

The sky above her went nova.

A burst of white light limned every flying drop of water into frozen perfection. The flash burned the image of Sam, mouth open with laughter, water flying from his brown hand, into her mind's eye forever.

Bea clenched her eyes shut reflexively as she flew backward, flung by an intense force that shuddered through air, water, and earth with a shock that changed the foundation of the world.

Nick woke to the sound of screaming.

The woman beside him emitted a sound like a fire alarm. The seat was bouncing so hard he would have hit his head on the ceiling if he hadn't been belted down. Nick tightened his hands on the armrests instinctively, realizing something else—there was no vibrating hum of engine noise. Nothing surrounded him but the sounds of people in terror. The plane was dropping so rapidly Nick's stomach felt like it was crawling up his throat.

At the front, near the cockpit, a flight attendant was yelling. "Tighten your seat belts and assume the crash position!"

"Holy crap," Nick whispered. This was really happening. They were going down. Nick couldn't remember what the crash position was; he'd never paid attention to the usual blah-de-blah at the beginning of the flight, and he looked around frantically. The woman beside him, still screaming, had leaned forward with her arms folded against the seat in front of her.

Like that was going to help.

They were dropping thirty thousand feet in a tin can with wings, and when they hit the water at this speed, it was going to be as hard as concrete.

Nick looked around, trying to spot the nearest exit, just in time to get hit in the head by the oxygen mask dropping down out of the ceiling. He put it on, keeping panic somewhere far away, the same detached place where he kept fear when he was getting in trouble on the dip.

They were descending at a steep downward angle, but as Nick looked out the window to the wing ahead, he could see the flaps were down. So they were trying to straighten out and descend as slowly as they could. Maybe there was a landing strip nearby?

Nick peered out the oval of window and could see the ocean below, vivid cobalt blue flecked with scudding whitecaps that were getting closer way too fast. No land anywhere that he could see. His heart began a roaring that filled his ears, drowning thought.

He heard the flight attendant yelling again, and the wails and screams subsided to listen.

"We're going to try to make it to Lanai. We've had some kind of power surge and have had a complete electrical failure, so our pilots are trying to bring the plane down at

44

enough of an angle to come up on the beach on the island. Be alert and prepared to help yourself and the passengers around you when we land!"

Nick had heard the tail was the safest place to be on a crashing plane, and he hoped it was true. He sat up straight, assessing the people around him, plotting a route to the nearest exit and mentally rehearsing his moves.

He wasn't going out like this. He was going to live.

The aircraft trembled, the metal shivered and moaned, and as the plane leveled off, the passengers' cries tapered off to sobbing. No lights were on anywhere, and the plane would have been dark but for windows with their shades up. A breathless tension gripped the passengers as they glided lower and lower, and suddenly the water was right beside the window and they were still going way too fast. Nick saw the leading edge of a wing catch on the surface, and with an agonized shriek the plane flipped over.

The world erupted in chaos as metal and human screams broke out, and they barreled forward upside down. Nick screamed, too, horror and rage filling his voice and echoing the chorus of destruction all around him.

This. This was it. This was all there would be, and it was so unfair.

Still upside down, he was hurled forward as if by a giant hand, and hit his head on the plastic seat back in front of him. Everything went black and silent.

6

EA OPENED HER EYES A moment—or maybe a lifetime—
later. She was prone on her back in the sand, her
legs in the water. The sky above her was on fire,
blinding white light banded with color swirling overhead
in hypnotizing patterns where the sky should have been.
The phenomena drowned out broad daylight, gloriously
beautiful.

Bea's brain seemed to have short-circuited. Something
major had just happened. Was it a bomb? She sat up.

"Sam!" He was floating face down in the water in front
of her. She thought she screamed, but she couldn't hear
anything other than a ringing in her ears. She surged up
and ran into the water, catching Sam under the armpits and
hauling him to shore. She whacked his back. He coughed
and spluttered, rolling over and sitting up to push sopping
hair out of his eyes.

She saw his mouth moving, thought he might have said,
"What happened?"

"We have to get to higher ground. Tsunami," she said, but she could tell by his blank expression that he couldn't hear, either. Everyone in Hawaii lived with the invisible threat of tsunami, tidal waves caused by underwater earthquakes. Maybe this had been an earthquake—or something more. She didn't remember the earth shaking, but something had sure knocked her flat.

She turned to look up onto the slope where Rainbow was yanking and bucking at her headstall but fortunately hadn't escaped. She jumped up and ran to the mare, cooing and soothing her, undoing the reins from the bush they'd tied her to.

"Come on, Sam!" she called to her brother. She couldn't hear her own voice, though she was pretty sure she was yelling as loud as she could because she felt her throat vibrating. Her brother stumbled toward her, smacking his ear, and Bea's eyes widened as she looked beyond him.

Trailing smoke, a passenger plane barreled toward them like a runaway locomotive.

Bea knew she must be screaming. She could feel her mouth stretching, the vibration of her throat, but still the world was silent as an antique horror movie set on slow motion.

The plane plowed into the ocean well behind Sam, raising a wall of water. It bounced like a skipped stone, flipping over and splashing down again, careening toward the reef.

Rainbow redoubled her efforts to escape. Bea barely held on to the reins, running alongside the mare and hauling herself up with a handful of mane as the panicked animal fled up the hill. She clamped onto the horse's heaving sides with her legs and hauled on one side of the reins to turn Rainbow's head, but there was no stopping the usually gentle animal. Rainbow blasted straight up the slope until exhaustion eventually brought her to a trembling, sweating halt.

That was the soonest Bea was able to turn the mare. She brought the horse around to look back down to the beach and see what they'd left behind.

"Bea! No!" Sam was yelling, but all he could hear was a thrumming in his ears as Rainbow hauled Bea farther up the hillside, the mare's glossy hindquarters churning up rocks and dirt. Something had scared the horse even more than the explosion or whatever it was. That was when Sam felt the earth shudder beneath his feet, knocking him sideways. He turned around to see something massive, metal, and looming, roaring silently toward him.

He scrambled away—straight up the hill, following the mare. He could feel his bad leg buckling and slipping but paid no attention—if he stopped, he was dead. He was sure of it.

Colors blurred in front of his eyes as he ran and ran and ran, breath sobbing through his lungs until a pain in his side stabbed him as he tripped and fell. This time he hugged the ground, feeling sweat burn his tightly closed eyes.

Gradually, the world stopped spinning and his lungs hurt a little less, the tearing sensation in his lungs subsiding. His nostrils filled with the smell of earth and something hot, like burning, a strange smell that tasted like metal at the back of his throat. Sam thought he might be able to hear something, a high-pitched sound, far off and fuzzy.

The hard red dirt felt like heaven against Sam's cheek because just this second, nothing bad was happening. He wasn't sure he was brave enough to look back at what had chased him, but finally he pushed himself up and turned to look back down the hill.

It was a big white plane.

A wing had broken off, leaving a spinning jet engine still attached to the cigar-shaped hulk that had landed upside down, covering the reef and halfway into their swimming hole.

He was surprised at how far he'd made it up the hill. He stood up and his legs wobbled. His side still hurt—a stitch, Mom used to call that.

People probably needed help in that plane. But he was scared now, and the fear felt like bands around his chest, chains on his arms and legs. He just wanted to get home to the house, get in bed and pull the covers up over his head. Maybe forever.

He looked around for Bea. Sure enough, she was coming back down the hill, still riding Rainbow. She could make that horse do anything.

He yelled "Bea!" She turned her head and saw him—maybe she could hear better than he could.

He knew she said "Sam!" as she slid off Rainbow, towing the mare as she ran to hug him in the hardest hug. He could smell her, a familiar comfort, and with his recent growth spurt, her cheek and his head collided. He could feel how skinny she was, like his arms could go around her twice. He was almost the same size as his big sister.

"We have to get help," she mouthed, standing back. He banged his ear again, but nothing happened except more ringing—it felt the same as when Dad whacked his head.

Someone had opened the door of the plane, and a few people climbed out, dropping into the waist-deep pool. Some seemed dazed, bleeding, staggering toward the beach, while a few turned to try to help the other passengers out the door.

Bea turned her head, her eyes scanning the area like she was looking for something, like she was listening. She did that a lot, and she reminded him of an owl, the native *pueo,* when she did. She said something, and he wasn't sure what, but it seemed like it was about getting help at Lanai City for the people on the plane.

"Okay." He didn't know what else to say. He was a kid with a bad leg. He couldn't help anybody—and it made him mad. He'd been feeling mad a lot lately, though there was nothing to do about it but keep trying.

Bea hopped up onto Rainbow and gave him a hand up to sit behind her on the hot, trembling horse. They kicked the mare into a trot back up the hill.

7

SOMETHING WAS VERY WRONG. NICK felt someone smacking his cheeks. His head felt like a giant water balloon. As consciousness formed, he realized it was because he was still hanging upside down, belted into his seat. The woman from beside him was kneeling below, reaching up, patting and pulling at him. "Oh, honey," she said. "You're alive."

Nick reached for his belt and realized he'd dump himself on his head. He took hold of the chair arm with one hand and released the belt with the other, and that slowed him down enough to sprawl into the space between the seats unharmed.

Chaos still reigned. Shouts and cries filled the jumbled space around him. Beside the window, waves beat on the side of the plane. Nick felt disoriented, trying to figure out what was going on. Was the plane under water?

"No, but this side of the plane is rotated over and submerged. We don't seem to be sinking, and people are getting out. Come on."

Nick must have spoken aloud, and for the first time he really looked at his seat companion. The woman had the freckled, crumpled skin of midlife, a brunette dye job showing white roots. She wore purple sweats with a teddy bear appliquéd on the front. She had the kind of warm brown eyes he'd seen on Labradors, and they were pleading with him as she tugged on his arm.

Nick shook his head, hoping to clear it, and moaned at the pain—his brain literally felt like it was sloshing. All around them, people were helping one another into the aisle and toward the front of the plane, but getting out was going slow.

"There's a door in the tail," Nick told the woman. "We should get it open. It might be easier to get out from this end, too."

She nodded. He retrieved his backpack and crawled past her to the open area where the food service carts had broken loose and tumbled into the aisle.

Nick felt his strength returning even as his head pounded from its impact with the seat back. He moved the carts aside, pulling and pushing the spilled and jumbled contents out of the way.

"What's your name?" the woman asked him. Nick paused as he reached the upside-down door, considering. This was his chance to assume another identity. Maybe now was the time to break away, make his move in the confusion of the accident. On the other hand, he hadn't even checked out his grandparents' situation yet. He could always switch identities later.

"Nick," he said. "And you?"

"Janice."

"Here it is, Janice," Nick said, gesturing her forward. "The door's upside down, but at least it's on the side above the water." Nick took hold of the metal handle and cranked it. It wouldn't move. Janice stood up beside him and put her weight onto it with his, and with a screech, the handle finally moved. Both of them put their shoulders into it and pushed the door. It slid down the outside of the plane, landing with a splash in the ocean.

Blinding sunlight, strobing with color, stabbed Nick's eyes. He cringed away. "So bright!"

"Something's off with that sunshine," Janice said. "I'm going to get some more people out this way. We still might blow up or something."

She hurried away while Nick reached up into the door opening, hauling his body up to sit on the tail of the plane and check the exit path.

The full extent of the wreck was revealed in blinding-bright, midday glory.

Straight ahead, a barren hulk of golden-brown island rose before Nick, the only real trees at the crown at the very top. The vast slope before him appeared to be arid grasses, stubble, and beach shrubs. The plane had come to rest on what must be a barrier reef, because another hundred feet of shallow turquoise water stretched before the twisted hulk of the plane. A long arc of deserted beach fronted them.

Getting down from this end of the plane was going to be a little hazardous. It would involve a slide down the side and landing in the sand-bottomed pool. Nick could hardly wait to splash into the water and leave this floating coffin behind—but he couldn't leave Janice alone to help others out of the wreck.

One of the wings floated like a raft on the side of the plane still in the water, gentle waves pushing the forlorn wreckage onto the reef. Up near the nose of the plane, Nick could see the flight crew helping others down out of the plane into waist-deep water, where they formed a straggling line heading for the shore. Already a cluster of people had gathered in the shade of shrubby trees growing at the top of the beach.

Noticeably absent were any emergency or rescue vehicles or the sound of sirens. In fact, there wasn't any man-made noise at all but the voices of the plane survivors, and those were muffled by the sound of breaking waves.

Nick dug his phone out of his pocket. It wouldn't even boot up, the screen stubbornly blank. From his elevated perch on the tail, he could see a dirt road running along the top of the beach. Scanning his surroundings, Nick spotted movement—a chestnut horse with two dark-haired kids on its bare back, cantering up the dirt road leading away from the site of the crash.

"Get help," Nick whispered, surprised to hear his own small voice in the ringing of his ears. "Please get help."

Then he turned and plunged back into the plane to help Janice bring out anyone who could navigate the exit.

Bea gave the horse a bucket of water and a restorative scoop of grain back at the house. The mare was too tired to ride straight to town even though the emergency with the plane beat at her brain with its urgency. Sam called from the front door, and this time she could hear his voice, though her hearing was still fuzzy.

"Bea, nothing works."

"What do you mean?"

"The lights. Clock, radio—nothing works."

Bea walked into the dim of the house, flicked the switch. "Maybe the batteries went out. I'll turn the generator on."

She went back outside to the little shed on the side of the house and worked the combination lock. Dad had always said the generator was the only thing they had that was worth stealing. She finally opened the door. The generator, a black Briggs & Stratton monstrosity, had a battery-powered ignition, and as she pushed the big red ON button, she wondered what the blast had been. A nuclear explosion? A devastating volcanic eruption was the most likely event for them to encounter here in Hawaii. But what kind of phenomena caused planes to fall out of the sky?

She stabbed the red button repeatedly, but nothing happened.

Sam looked over her shoulder. "Maybe new batteries for the ignition switch?"

"Just what I was thinking." She hurried into the kitchen and fetched a couple of AA batteries, returned and installed them in the switch box. She hit the red button again, and this time a spark flew out of the button area with a fizzing sound.

Still no ignition.

Sam had brought a screwdriver, and when she stood back, he inserted the small Phillips-head into the switch box and unscrewed the metal surround. Running from the contact points of the batteries were red ignition wires—and they were frayed, the plastic melted.

She and Sam put their heads farther into the shed and checked all around the generator—every bit of wire that could have carried a charge was damaged. Bea stepped back, putting her hands on her hips and watching her brother. Sam had always had a mechanical knack, and now, when he turned to her, his face was pinched with anxiety.

"All this wiring is shot. It's lucky the whole thing didn't catch on fire." Sam pointed to a scrim of black charcoal on the wall behind the generator. "I wonder what's happening in the town."

"Oh my God." Bea's heart bumped against her ribs, and she clapped a hand over her mouth. "Jaden. I wonder if he's okay. And Dad." She turned and ran back into the house, tearing off her bathing suit in the bedroom to haul on some jeans and a T-shirt. She braided her hair as she went back into the kitchen, rubber-banding the damp, salty strands.

She threw all the food she could find into a box and carried it outside.

"Sam, we need to get ready for a lot of things to happen. People could come here looking for shelter and food—and we don't know if they'll be friendly. I'm going back to town to see what's happening, see what I can find out and look for Dad. You take all the food you can out to the cave and then keep an eye out. If anyone comes, hide."

"Why don't we help them?"

"Maybe we will. But this could be bad if the explosion or whatever fried all the electricity."

"You're not leaving me here." Sam's brown eyes narrowed and he set his jaw. She didn't remember seeing that expression on him before, but it looked remarkably like her own face when she made up her mind about something. "Let's go together."

It might be time to quit babying Sam. "Okay. Let's hurry, then. I just hate to leave the house unguarded."

"We'll lock it."

Bea snorted. "Like that will matter."

Even as they spoke, the two had gone into the kitchen, and Bea took a plastic garbage bag and threw bedding and clothes into it while Sam filled plastic gallon jugs they used for filtering water. In half an hour they'd taken everything that seemed like it might be useful out to the cave. She arranged some old lumber their dad had been using for firewood over the cave opening.

Bea felt her heart pounding with urgency as she belted the riding blanket onto the mare. She hopped up, her .22 rifle in one hand. Rainbow tossed her head and snorted as Bea gave Sam a hand up behind her—she could tell the mare was tired, but the rest and food had restored her somewhat.

"Let's go, girl." She clucked and dug her heels in. Sam wrapped his arms around her waist, and they trotted up the road toward Lanai City.

They smelled the smoke of burning long before they came to the town.

8

BEA AND SAM TIED RAINBOW and climbed up onto the flat stone platform with its bird's-eye view down into Lanai City. On their bellies, instinctively keeping out of sight, Bea and Sam crawled forward and looked off the edge of the rock.

The town, set in a cuplike hollow surrounded by tall Cook pines and raised ground, was obscured by billowing smoke, intermittently clearing to reveal flames blanketing it. Bea's hearing was still off, but she could make out a crazy crackle. The smell wasn't the clean of wood smoke; it was plastic, paint, and metal salted by gas.

The terrible scene was strangely silent. Bea realized she was listening for sirens—fire and police—but there were none. Just the crackling roar of the town, eerily burning.

"I have to go down there," Bea said. "But I'd feel better if you stayed. You can keep an eye on me from here."

Sam was silent for a long moment. Unspoken between them was how hard it was for Sam to move fast on foot, and packing double was a burden to the mare.

"Okay. Find help for the plane people first, and look for Dad." Sam reached into his back pocket and took out the wicked metal Y of his slingshot with its built-in wrist support, industrial-grade rubber thong, and pouch of small round lead fishing weights. Their father had offered him a pellet gun, but Sam preferred hunting with the slingshot. Bea had seen one of those little lead weights tear the head right off of a grouse.

"I'm going to take the rifle," Bea said to Sam. "Lie low if you see anyone you don't know. People are going to be scared and maybe they won't be thinking straight. We don't know yet, so stay out of sight."

"I will." Sam gave her a fierce hug. "Get help. Come back as soon as you can."

"Of course." She hugged him back. On her way back down to Rainbow, she put her hand into the secret crack in the stones where Jaden left her notes.

Sure enough, there was a folded paper. She unfolded it to read Jaden's scrawl.

The news says the lights are a solar storm, he wrote. *Hopefully, it will just be a pretty light show, but people are scared. I will bring gas next time. Everyone is buying it all, and I couldn't get any.* He'd folded twenty dollars into the middle of the note. *Your cut of the money. See you soon.*

Bea slid the note and cash into her hip pocket, wondering when it would be useful. This disaster seemed all encompassing, and what was twenty dollars going to do? Yesterday it would have meant so much.

Bea untied the mare, pulled herself up, and swung the horse in an arc, kicking her into a canter down the road toward the burning town, the rifle balanced on her thigh.

Sam watched his sister ride away like she were part of the horse, the rifle upright as a spear. Bea reminded him of pictures he'd seen of warriors riding into battle. The mare seemed to have found some new reservoir of energy, unleashing a full gallop toward the town. Gouts of smoke rolled across the road, and then horse and rider were engulfed, disappearing from sight.

Sam scooted back from the edge and rolled onto his back. The sky was clear again, a mocking blue bowl. Like nothing bad had happened. Like no airplanes had fallen out of the sky right in front of him. Even the sparkles in the sky were gone.

He put his arms over his eyes, stinging from the smoke—and let himself cry. What if Bea never came back? And his dad was gone? He'd be left here, alone. Just getting back to the house would take hours with his bad leg, and then what?

He sobbed harder, a storm of weeping that cried out all that was wrong with the world. Finally, winding down, he rolled over and leaned his hot, throbbing face on the stone. His head hurt and his stomach churned.

He missed his mom with a fierce ache—she'd known how to fold him into a hug that made everything feel better.

You're not alone. Bea will come back.

A voice, deep and ringing, sounded in his inner ear. Sam gulped down his tears, scrubbed them off his face, and wiped his nose on his T-shirt sleeve. He pushed himself up to look around.

Someone had just spoken to him; he was sure of it.

The smoke had gusted away from the road for a moment. The town was still burning, and Bea was still gone.

Have a little faith, the voice in his mind said. *You're not alone.*

Sam rubbed his stinging eyes. Even at a distance he recognized Bea's friend Jaden Acupan emerging out of the smoke, coming down the road toward the stone outcrop. Jaden was wearing a backpack, moving at a jog, and carrying a spear gun. Sam pushed away from the edge. Surely Bea didn't mean for him to hide from her best friend. He scrubbed his face again and climbed down the rock to meet Jaden.

"Thank God you're here." Jaden's dark eyes scanned around and behind Sam as he came to a halt. Sweat, dirt, and smoke wreathed his shirt and swim trunks. Whipcord lean but filled out in the shoulders, Jaden radiated an adult competency that brought prickling tears of relief to Sam's eyes. "My dad sent me to look for you guys. Where's Bea? And what happened to your face?"

"She rode into town to try to find help and to look for Dad. And I fell."

"Fell. Right." Jaden's voice conveyed both kindness and disbelief as he squeezed Sam's shoulder. He swiveled on his heel, looking back down the road. "Dammit—I mean darn, she shouldn't have done that. It's not safe."

"What do you mean?" Sam gulped.

Jaden looked back at him. "Did she say where she was going?"

"We saw a plane fall out of the sky. She was going to try to find some help for the survivors. They're down at the beach." Jaden must have seen the distress in his face, because he slung an arm around Sam's shoulders, turned him, and headed toward the rock.

"Does she have the .22?"

"Yes. And she's on Rainbow."

"She'll be fine, then, but I don't know how she's going to find anyone who can help. Everyone's swamped trying to put out the fires. Let's keep a lookout. So, tell me about the plane." They both lay on their bellies and watched the road as Sam told his halting tale from the top of the rock.

"It looked like people might have died, and there were a lot of injuries," Sam finished. "What got the fire going in town?"

"The fire started when the transformers blew, which happened right after the explosion," Jaden said. "Every house must have just sprouted sparks from the outlets, and a lot of them went up right away." He cleared his throat. "It's not good. My family sent me to find you guys, see if we can scrounge for food and hide it in your cave. Things are going to get bad pretty fast, and not everyone's helping one another like they should."

"We wanted to get help for the people from the plane."

"Well, I don't think that's going to be possible. None of the emergency vehicles are running. I did bring some first aid supplies in my backpack, but I don't know how much good it will do. Our house hasn't burned so far because our friends and family are helping keep the neighbors' houses from going up, hoping it doesn't spread to our block."

"I hope Bea comes back soon," Sam said. He couldn't put his fears for his sister into words.

"Me too," Jaden said. They stared down the road into the flames.

Nick helped the last person through the water to the beach, lowering the elderly lady to the sand in the shade of one of the beach trees. She collapsed, weeping. Her husband was one of the six dead passengers lined up in a battered, bloody row on the beach, their faces covered with blankets from the plane. He patted her shoulder, looking around for help—where was Janice? Comforting old ladies was definitely not his thing. He stood and turned away, but she clutched his sleeve. "Don't leave me!"

Nick spotted Janice up under the trees, working on one of the injured passengers. He counted ten hurt people lying on towels and airline blankets in a row. His back ached from carrying the bodies out of the plane to the beach and helping with the injured, and smears of blood already stiffened his clothes. He shut his eyes hard for a moment to block the memories of what he'd had to see, and touch, and do.

It didn't work.

For something to do, the habit powerful, Nick took his cell phone out and tried to power it on with his thumb.

No cell phones were working. They'd been unable to contact help because nothing worked, not even the radio on the plane. Listening to the adults speculating, Nick had a feeling they were on their own, that the explosion that had thrown them out of the sky had affected a lot more than just their plane. As he looked around at his bewildered, traumatized fellow passengers, he realized he was doing better than most in spite of his persistent headache.

He sat down beside the grief-stricken woman and unzipped his backpack. He took out a bottle he'd purchased in the airport. "Here, have some water." He looped an arm around her trembling shoulders, realizing it had been a long time since he'd helped anyone.

Bea reined in the mare as a rolling boil of smoke engulfed them. Rainbow's ears flattened, and she snorted, tossing her head in discomfort. Bea leaned forward to lay her cheek alongside the horse's neck.

"Easy does it, girl." Bea looked at the ground below them. Visibility was terrible, until another gust of wind lifted the smoke, swirling it away in the opposite direction. The crackling she'd heard increased to a roar, and Bea could feel the heat.

Rainbow slowed to a walk, bobbing her head anxiously, as they approached the first of the burning houses. Bea could hear shouts, and through the smoke she glimpsed a chain of shadowy people passing buckets and tossing water on a house—not one of the burning ones, one of those beside it. It appeared that without real firefighting equipment available, folks were focusing on keeping the fire from spreading.

A dog darted out in front of them, appearing suddenly out of the murk and barking. Rainbow shied, a sideways leap that nearly unseated Bea. The horse wheeled and galloped back the way they'd come.

Just as well—at the moment, it didn't look like she'd be able to find anyone able to leave firefighting to help the plane-wreck victims. The hotel was up a slight incline, just outside of town, and that's where Bea needed to look for Dad. She let the horse run, knowing how tired the mare was. She reminded the mare she wasn't alone with soothing words in her flattened ear.

The exhausted horse finally slowed. Shudders ran over Rainbow's hide as though it were crawling with ants. Bea slid down to the ground, patting the mare's neck as she walked her up the long, uphill-sloping hotel driveway lined with majestic pines. The drive ended at a circle turnaround and a gracious edifice styled after a plantation mansion.

The Lanai Lodge was everything gracious and high-toned, backed by a rolling golf course, putting green, walking trails, multiple pools, and an orchid-filled greenhouse.

And it was on fire, too.

Bea sped up beside the mare, heading past the extension of the Lodge under giant banyan trees. The building burned merrily, with no suppression efforts in sight. As they hit the springy, manicured grass of the grounds, she finally saw someone—a coworker of her father's. The man's eyes were wide, and he was streaked with soot and dirt, his stare glazed as he hurried past them.

"Mr. Inciong! You seen my dad? Will Whitely?"

"Got to get home to my family," Inciong tossed over his shoulder. "He took his truck down to the docks to pick up some supplies before the explosion."

The docks were a long, winding way down the hump of the island. Her father could be stranded anywhere outside of town along the precipitous two-lane road that switchbacked to the harbor.

One harbor was where the passenger ferry docked, along with tour boats and sightseeing catamarans. A few miles around the coast, on the "backside" of the island, was a working harbor accommodating the more plebeian transport boats that supplied Lanai. He'd probably gone to the supply harbor, a long and strenuous trek for Rainbow. The mare was in no shape to attempt it at the moment. Bea turned to call after Mr. Inciong, but the man had broken into a run, no doubt glimpsing the fire in town and terrified for his family.

There was no one to help the plane survivors and no way for her to communicate their emergency. Rainbow needed water, and Bea's own throat felt raw and sandpapery.

Around the back corner of the hotel, a line of people was trying to stop the fire. Motel guests in flowered resort wear and golf shoes were scooping buckets of water out of the swimming pools and reflecting ponds and passing them hand-to-hand to toss on the walls of the main lodge area. Several men with fire axes were chopping through the glass and wood of the connecting breezeway between the two sections of the Lodge—they must have decided the section where the rooms were located couldn't be saved.

Even as Bea watched, the flames on that building shot higher, catching in the limbs of the beautiful overarching banyan tree. The leaves darkened, curled, and floated away, obscene black snowflakes.

Bea couldn't bear to look, and there was nothing she could do. It was the same horrible feeling she'd had watching the plane wreck. Rainbow tugged toward one of the ponds, where swans and ducks quacked and milled in panic at the far end. Bea walked the mare over, and the horse sank her mouth in, sucking up water.

Bea splashed water onto her hot, gritty face and hands, but she couldn't drink the pond water. She looked around and spotted a spigot, ran over and turned it on. Nothing came out.

Bea thought rapidly—the only water that would be running would be what was self-contained or entirely gravity-fed, like toilet tanks, which would be good for one flush. She knew where the employee lounge for the groundskeepers was, and there was a gravity-fed water dispenser there.

When Rainbow had drunk her fill, Bea tossed a few handfuls of water onto the hot horse and picked up the rifle. She wondered why she'd bothered with the .22. It was tricky to carry, and so far the only people she'd seen had been terrified or occupied.

But bad things would come later. She was sure of it.

The mare bobbed her head with fatigue and nerves as they walked across the manicured putting green toward a discreetly painted storage barn. The utilitarian building was screened by gracious plantings and housed lawn mowers and equipment.

Bea reached the steel-sided building and knocked on the door. "Hello? Anyone here?" She jiggled the handle and pushed the door wide. "Hello?"

The break room was empty of people, but the plastic folding table, ringed by molded chairs, was covered with half-empty cups of coffee, open water bottles, and hands of cards scattered over the table and across the floor. Several of the lightweight chairs were upended.

Bea pictured the employees on break, playing a hand of cards, eating malasadas from a pink box in the center of the table—and the event happening, knocking them flying. The electrical outlets were all surrounded by telltale burn marks, but because the building was metal, it hadn't caught fire.

She tied Rainbow's reins to a tree branch and leaned the rifle against the building nearby. Inside the break room, Bea picked up a plastic water bottle from a rack of them beside the big five-gallon water bottle on a dispenser. That water was going to be very important to the people working up a sweat outside the burning hotel. In the meantime, she drank the entire bottle she'd found and refilled it.

Casting about the room for useful objects, Bea wolfed down several of the Portuguese malasadas, slightly stale but still delicious—sugar-dusted, deep-fried dough balls filled with sweet, creamy haupia pudding. She found a cloth shopping bag and stowed several water bottles, two malasadas wrapped in napkins for Sam, some pruners, and a pair of leather gloves.

"What are you doing here?" A man's voice, sharp as the crack of a whip, came from the doorway. Bea gulped, swallowing the last of a malasada in a hard lump, and swung the cloth bag onto her shoulder as she turned to face the question.

"Looking for my dad," she said, glancing at the backlit shadow of an adult blocking the door. "I was just leaving."

"You mean looting." Icy tones of disapproval as she approached him. The man was obviously a hotel guest, his lavender polo shirt streaked with soot, beefy face red from exertion.

Bea decided not to answer and strode forward.

"Hey!" He shot out an arm, blocking her. "We need help. We need all the supplies we can get. Give me that bag."

Bea had left the rifle leaning against the doorframe outside, and panic seized her at the thought of losing it.

"No! My little brother needs help, too." She flung his arm up. He tried to grab the bag as she passed, but she swung away, moving fast to scoop up the rifle, which he fortunately hadn't seen. She headed for the mare, hidden by the side of the building.

"Hey!" he yelled, coming after her. "We need that horse!"

Bea yanked the reins loose and Rainbow sidled away, nervous at the raised voices and the man's reaching hands. Bea leaped up onto her back, but the man had hold of Rainbow's bridle.

"Nothing personal," he huffed, hauling on the reins as Bea pulled them the other way. "We just need this horse."

"Nothing personal," Bea replied, releasing the reins to raise the rifle, sighting down its barrel to his sturdy midsection. "She's mine."

The man yanked again. "You wouldn't."

"I won't kill you. But it will hurt and will probably get infected."

Bea could hardly believe that the low, flat voice threatening a man with bodily harm was her own. Slowly he let go of the reins and the headstall, smoke-reddened eyes reading her intent as he backed away, hands raised.

"Good choice." Bea used her legs to turn the mare, not lowering the gun until they were cantering away across the manicured grounds. She reached forward to catch the flapping reins, but Rainbow was spooked now, unused to the lashing, loose leather. The mare galloped across the golf course, headed out of town.

Bea leaned forward, talking to the animal, one hand clutching her mane, the rifle in the other. Darned gun had finally earned its keep. "C'mon, girl. All this running is tiring you out. Just take it easy. We're okay."

Rainbow tossed her head in agreement, snorting, and slowed to a walk. Bea was able to slide off and catch hold of the headstall, bringing the mare to a stop.

Bea tilted her head to look at the sky—she couldn't even see a sparkle of leftover phosphorescence in the deepening blue of evening. "Let's go back to the rock and see what Sam's been up to."

She walked beside the horse, giving the mare a rest as she looked back at the hotel. One side of the two-part structure was completely gone, the flames catching the banyan trees on fire. It appeared that the guests had succeeded in separating the two buildings, because the main lodge was not yet burning.

Bea wondered how long the water in the break room would last for all those people. This morning, that man's biggest problem had been avoiding a sunburn while golfing—and in just a few hours, he was willing to assault her and steal her horse.

And she'd been willing to shoot him if he did.

9

NICK HAD MET SOME YOUNG people as they finished hauling the last of the food and water out of the plane, along with all the carry-on bags. Kelly, Amos, Kevin, Mike, Ricky, Ashley, and Zunc, all late teens and early twenties, had hurled themselves into helping, and now they'd finished dumping the contents of the bags into a pile, pulling out anything that might be useful for the group as the adults sprawled in shocked exhaustion along the beach.

The sun had set in a bonfire of vivid color, though the spectacular effects they'd seen when the plane went down were gone. A chill wind blew up across the purpling ocean. Nick's stomach cramped with hunger. He'd already eaten a crumpled plastic tray of cold meat loaf and drunk the last of a bottle of water.

"I think I should go up the road, try to find some people," Nick said to his companions. It wasn't his usual mode to make a suggestion like this and stand out in a crowd—but this situation was extraordinary. He couldn't stop thinking about going up the road, seeing where those kids with the horse had gone. He had to try to find help for the injured and food and shelter for the rest of the survivors.

Kevin, a bleached-blond Australian surfer traveling with his sister, Ashley, stood up from where he was sorting one of the suitcases. "I was just waiting for someone to say that. This is Lanai, not an uninhabited atoll. I mean, I don't know why no one's come to help us, but it seems like it's time to find out."

It wasn't long before their little band set off up the road in the light of the moon, with promises to return in the morning at the very latest. Nick was glad of the cool darkness as they hiked up the steep, switchbacked road rising to the highest point of the island. About halfway up, he spotted a dirt side road, leading to some sort of residence that was hidden by the darkness. An hour later, soaked with sweat, legs trembling, Nick stood with the other young crash survivors, gazing down at the conflagration that was Lanai City.

"Well, now we know why no one's come looking for us," Kevin said.

"Oh my God." Ashley had tears in her voice as she drew close to her brother. "What are we going to do now?"

"I don't think we should bother going down there," Zune said. "They won't be able to help us, and we'll just get in the way."

"We should go down tomorrow when we can see, and find people to talk to," Nick said. "I saw a side road leading to a house back down a ways. Why don't we see if they can shelter us for the night."

"Good idea," Kevin said. They filed back down the road.

"I'm so tired." Ashley started crying. The girls banded together, arms around each other. Nick walked a little faster ahead, wondering how he'd somehow become a leader in this little band. Dodger would have told him to melt into the darkness and find his own way, but Nick had a feeling that surviving now might depend on having the right friends.

The house was a silent, dark hulk, hunched and waiting in the deepest shadow under tall trees. Kevin went up onto the porch first, knocking loudly on the door. "Hello? Anyone home?" Kevin persisted at this while Nick went around the back, finding a screen door.

"Hello?" Nick called. No sound, no movement, no light of any kind. Nick tested the handle. Locked. He picked up a heavy rock near the steps, and a couple of bashes later, the door handle fell off. He pulled the screen door open. There was no further barrier, and his heart pounding, he tiptoed into the dark house.

It smelled ever so faintly of fish, and his footsteps creaked on old wooden floors. He crept forward, feeling his way. "Anybody home?"

No answer. The place had a feeling to it, an empty echo that confirmed the residents were gone. Nick made his way to the front door and unlocked it for the rest of the group. "No one's here," he said. "We might as well spend the night here."

Sam and Jaden stared down the road, flat on their bellies, chins resting on folded arms. It seemed like they had been waiting like that for hours. Sam sneaked a glance at Jaden. The sixteen-year-old's head had rotated to the side, his mouth slightly ajar. He'd fallen asleep.

Jaden must have been really tired. He said he'd been passing buckets of water ever since the fire broke out, until his father pulled him off the line and sent him to find the two of them. Sam looked back at the town—the smoke had thinned quite a bit, and he could see that about a third of Lanai City was gone, nothing but black shells marking the shapes of homes and cars.

The billows of smoke were lit from within with an otherworldly glow. Darkness gathered and thickened across the battered area. Emerging from those shadows, Sam spotted the silhouette of a horse—and walking beside the mare, the slender shape of his sister.

"She's coming back!" He shook Jaden's arm. "Jaden, she's back!" He scrambled backward across the rock and clambered down—his foot never slowed him climbing—and he hit the ground at a run. He reached Bea first, throwing his arms around her, noticing she was damp and smelled of smoke and pond water.

Bea squeezed him back, and he felt her look up at Jaden, the shift of her attention. "Thanks for keeping an eye on my brother."

"You're welcome. What did you find?"

"I think I know where Dad went, and I want to go look for him. Rainbow is played out, though. I have to send her home with Sam."

Sam tightened his arms. "No! You can't go back into town alone!"

"Yeah, Bea. Bad idea."

"Not an option. I had word he took the truck to town. He could be hurt."

"Then I'll go back with you—my brothers could help."

"But what about Sam—and Rainbow? Someone tried to steal her. I want to get her out of town. And Sam…"

"I can take Rainbow home myself," Sam said, pulling away from his sister. She was treating him like a handicapped kid—and he was sick of it.

Rainbow's head hung low, and her sides were streaked with sweat. He reached for the reins, took them from his sister, and felt rather than saw Bea and Jaden trying to figure out what to do. He gave a tug on the leather. "Come, Rainbow."

The tired animal followed him without protest as he led her back up the road. He squelched the fear rising up like bile. His bad foot already ached. There were several more miles to go, but he wasn't going to be treated like a baby. He could help, too.

A moment later he felt Jaden's hand on his shoulder. "Let me give you a boost up. Rainbow can carry a lightweight like you without even noticing." The mare gave a snort but no further objection as Jaden boosted Sam onto the horse, and he couldn't help being relieved not to be walking as he settled onto the riding blanket and rearranged the reins.

Sam looked back. Bea had already disappeared, back the way she'd come. The darkness closed over the smoking town, flickers of red the only illumination. "Why did you let her go?"

"She's going to my house to get my brothers. She's got the gun—it'll be okay. I just wanted to go where the food was."

"Yeah, right," Sam said. "She's making you babysit me."

"What? You kidding? Actually, she told me she's worried the people from the plane will find the house and take it over."

A new fear emerged, one he realized had always been there.

All those people—hurt, hungry, and thirsty. Where would they go when they realized no one was coming to help them? They'd walk until they found the road—a steep blacktop ribbon leading to the spine of the island and Lanai City—and a rutted two-lane track that came off it going straight to their house. Fortunately, the house wasn't visible from the road, but still …

Sam kicked Rainbow's sides. "C'mon, girl! We have to get home!" The mare rolled an eye and walked slightly faster, but that was all.

Sam liked Rainbow, and the horse tolerated him—but he was no Bea to be obeyed.

"Let's just hurry." Jaden shifted his spear gun to his shoulder. "And hope no one's broken in."

Bea broke into a jog back toward town. The dark wrapped her in dubious protection, and she was grateful for it even if her footing was uncertain on the asphalt road. She was wearing rubber slippers—hardly the right footwear for trekking through rubble from a fire.

I will lead you to him. Her 'aumakua sent her a mental picture of her dad's truck, crashed in a ravine on the way down to the industrial harbor. Bea hurried faster, her heart squeezing, wondering, as she often did, if Beosith was just her stressed-out imagination at work. It didn't really matter. She didn't have any better idea where to go.

The explosion could have caused the truck's engine to fail, because everywhere along the road, automobiles were pulled over and abandoned. Once again Bea wondered what kind of disaster had befallen them—it seemed to have ruined everything that relied on electricity.

Jaden had handed her a piece of rope from his backpack in that moment of communication they'd shared as Sam led the tired horse away. She remembered the intensity of his shadowed dark eyes as he'd grasped her shoulders and how he'd leaned toward her. For a moment she'd thought he was going to kiss her, and there was no denying the disappointment she'd felt as he just leaned in close, his breath tickling her ear and lifting the hair on the back of her neck. "Get my brothers to help you. Be careful."

Bea thought of a use for the rope and stopped to slip a knot over the hard resin stock of the .22 rifle and another half hitch over the barrel, with slack in between. She slung the gun over her shoulder with the makeshift strap. She still carried the cloth sack holding a water bottle, pruners, gloves, and the malasadas.

Bea knew she might as well eat the malasadas. She was going to need energy—but her stomach churned, imagining her father trapped in the cab of the wrecked truck. He hadn't always been the violent, drinking, paranoid man he'd become. He'd always worked hard and had been a little stern—but he used to know how to laugh. When their mother was alive, he'd been a good dad.

Sometimes she still glimpsed love in his chambray-blue eyes. Losing Angel seemed to have broken something in him. She wouldn't blame him for any of it, if it weren't for how he treated Sam.

She slowed to walk through the town. The part of the village closest to the hotel had fared the worst. Whole blocks of the modest wooden homes, roofed in tin, were nothing but smoking rubble now. The smell of the smoke was a sharp, sour tang, painful in her nostrils. A dog barked from a driveway, and she saw campfires and lanterns with people clustered around them in the yards and houses that remained.

Her rubber slippers crunched over cinders and rubble in the road. She broke into a trot, making her way into the unburned portion of town and up Jaden's street. His house, a small green cube with white trim and a corrugated tin roof, was black but for the glow of a lamp in the kitchen window.

Bea started up the walkway, a path lined with ocean-worn stones from the beach, and glimpsed the scene inside the window. Jaden's family was holding hands, heads bowed in prayer around the dining room table. Bowls set before each person steamed.

Bea stood looking at the peaceful scene, feeling a longing deeper than jealousy.

There was no question that the Apucan family would come and help her, but this was her errand. They'd worked hard, they'd survived, and so had their house. The least she could do was let them have a restful evening for as long as that lasted.

She wished there were some way to let them know that Jaden was safe, that they'd found each other—but there wasn't, without creating a scene she wouldn't be able to leave.

Bea turned and walked quietly back to the main road.

Outside the town, the night sky flared into a million snowflake bits of starlight, and Bea craned her neck, looking for any trace of the phenomena, which seemed to have completely disappeared. She hadn't realized until it was gone how even the minor light pollution of Lanai City washed out the vault of celestial gems.

Bea kept moving, her heart thumping with exertion—and tension. What if she rescued her father just so she could then try to manage him while keeping Sam safe? Still, he was strong, knowledgeable, and a grown-up. He was all the family they had now that the rest of their relatives were inaccessible on Molokai. And maybe this crisis would bring out the dad he used to be—if he was even still alive.

The spot where the truck had gone off the road was hard to see in the dim light. The road had begun its narrow descent to the working harbor. It ran along a dry gulch filled with boulders and a few scraggly guava trees, a gulch Bea knew well in the daytime—but now all dark mystery.

Bea spotted the crushed lantana bushes that a vehicle had driven over as it left the road, lit by the light of the rising moon. The woody, drought-resistant shrubs had already partly sprung back up. Bea clung to one of the bushes and looked over the cliff into the black depths.

Her stomach cramped as she realized how unrealistic it was for her to do anything to actually rescue her father. She regretted not bringing the Apucans, after all.

Bea scanned the darkness of the gulch and didn't spot the truck until the white glow of the moon picked out a reflection of taillights.

"Oh God. Please let him be alive," Bea said. "Dad! Are you down there?" she shouted. Her voice bounced back at her.

There was no answer. She called again. Her heart pounded now, a band of terror tight around her chest. She couldn't imagine how he could be okay. If he were able, he'd have tried to get back to them.

Bea cast about for something to tie the rope to—it was only about twenty feet long, but it would have to do for the first sharp drop at the top of the cliff. She could probably climb down the rest. She tied one end of the rope around the sturdy metal post of the guardrail—a guardrail that hadn't extended far enough around the curve of the road to stop the trajectory of her father's truck.

Bea yanked on the knot tied to the metal post one more time and slipped off her rubber slippers. She emptied the cloth bag of all but the pruners, water, and food, which might be useful, and set the rifle and other contents under a bush in case anyone came by. She pulled on the leather gloves and carefully lowered herself off the edge of the cliff.

10

GRAVEL AND DIRT FROM THE crumbling cliff edge bit into Bea's abdomen as she pushed herself out into space, wrapping the rope between her thighs and holding on to it with both hands. She wished the gloves were smaller—they seemed to roll on her hands, affording little protection, and all that kept her from falling was her grip on the rough hemp.

You can do this. It's only a little way to where you can put your feet on the rocks, Beosith said in her mind.

She swiveled and swung in the darkness as she tried to move down, and a hysterical laugh threatened to explode— Beosith, her guardian angel `aumakua, was all that was keeping her going. His very existence made her sanity questionable.

"I'm too old for an imaginary friend," she muttered, and could swear she heard a dragonly snort in her mind.

The moment of terror and hysteria passed. She scooted down the rope, feeling it burning the sensitive skin of her inner thighs even through her jeans, but she lowered herself a few more feet, reaching for a boulder with her toes. Bea's hands cramped and her arms trembled as her foot fumbled in space, reaching for the rock. Her bare foot found it, settling onto the rough, still-warm surface. She cautiously transferred her weight from the rope to the boulder and let go of the line.

From there, she climbed down, foot by careful foot, to the bottom of the gulch.

The truck was wedged hood-first between two large boulders whose bulk partly hid it. Bea couldn't see anything in the dark and felt her way down the side of the Ford to the front of the cab.

"Dad? Dad!"

Bea felt along the side to the bent but unobstructed door. She grabbed the handle and yanked. Nothing happened. The window was open, and she moved up, bracing herself to look inside.

A welter of white airbag hid the steering wheel, but the cab of the truck was empty.

"Dad!" she cried, looking up, around. The sound of her voice bounced off the rocks. "Where are you?"

I don't know.

Find him!

No. I helped you with this, but that isn't my mission. I'm here to help you.

Helping me is finding him! The thought of the climb back up the cliff was just too much for Bea right now. She climbed into the front seat and sat in the padded plastic space that had held her father's body.

There was a weird chemical smell from the airbag, but she could smell him in there, too, that tang of sweat and booze that had become such a part of her father. She looked around in the dim glow of moonlight. There was no blood, so he hadn't been injured.

Will Whitely's battered metal lunch box had fallen against the opposite door, and the John Deere hat lay on top of it.

"Dad's alive." All Bea's conflicted feelings for her father rose up in a tangled, inarticulate ball to choke her. For the first time she felt all the tiny wounds of the day, burns from flying cinders, abrasions from the rope, soreness from all that riding—and a deep, abiding tiredness. Tears prickled her eyes, stinging like ant bites.

"I'm just going to rest a minute," she said aloud, wadding the airbag into a pillow to rest on. A feeling of protective reassurance came from the *mo'o* dragon.

I'll be watching over you.

Sam felt like the trek back to the house through the dark would never end. Even on horseback, he was tired and sore and kept nodding off. Beginning to slide off the mare jerked him awake repeatedly, and he snapped upright again when he felt Jaden's hand on his leg. Rainbow had come to a halt, her head hanging.

"Get off, Sam."

Sam slid down. His bad leg buckled, and he caught himself by leaning on the mare, her warm horsey smell filling his nostrils. The moon was a pale round, rising behind Molokai along with a cache of stars. Last night's ribbons of light had disappeared.

Sam could tell by Jaden's tense silence and the tight hand on his shoulder that the older boy was on high alert. They had stopped outside the stand of trees that marked the Whitely house. "Let's leave Rainbow here. Move up quiet to the house and check it out," Jaden whispered.

"Okay." Sam slid the bridle over Rainbow's ears and dropped the bit out of her mouth. The mare chomped in relief as he kept the bridle over her head and pushed it back around her neck, a makeshift noose. He tied the leather reins to a bush, turned back, and unbuckled the strap that held the riding blanket onto her back, and slid it off. It was damp with sweat, and he draped it over another bush. "Bea would want me to rub her down."

"We can do that later, if the house is empty," Jaden said. "Follow me and stay quiet. We'll get closer and see what's up."

Sam imitated Jaden's hunched posture as they moved into the stand of avocado and mango trees that had been planted fifty years ago when the house was built. The boys walked as carefully as they could through crunching leaves—but even somewhere as familiar to Sam as the grove had now become a foreign land peopled by bogeymen in the dark.

Sam bumped into Jaden's back. In the shadow of the mango closest to the house, Sam peered around the older boy to see what had brought him to a halt.

There was a light in the window.

"Damn," Jaden whispered. "I mean, shoots. You didn't leave a light on, did you?"

"Nothing was working," Sam whispered back. "The generator was broken; all the wiring was melted."

"Looks like a candle or a lamp. Someone's inside."

11

SAM FELT HIS THROAT CLOSE as tears threatened. He was so tired. He just wanted to go home, get in his bed, and sleep for a week. Oh—and maybe have a little water, too. And some food would be nice.

"Stay here, Sam. I'll try to sneak closer and see if I can tell how many there are." Jaden didn't wait to see if Sam obeyed—the older boy just shifted forward and was gone, elusive as a moth.

Sam leaned his cheek against the rough bark of the mango tree. He stuffed down his tiredness and anger—there was something he could do, too. They'd have to hide Rainbow somewhere. She couldn't stay tied up with her bridle for long—and she was sure to need water. Jaden wouldn't know where her tie-out rope was, or her water bucket. Fortunately, the lean-to shelter where they were stored was away from the house.

Sam mustered his energy and sneaked to the edge of the grove, where the barbed-wire fence of Rainbow's paddock began. There was no cover in the paddock, but scudding clouds had moved over the moon. He had to chance it.

Sam slid between the barbed-wire strands as he'd done a hundred times and trotted across the dusty paddock. No one shouted and no cry came from the house. He made it to the shed where they fed Rainbow, and she got out of the elements. Coiled against the back wall was a halter and tie-out rope for when they moved her around to eat grass. Sam took that and picked up her water bucket.

They'd have to get water, and that could be a problem. But he only had room in his brain for one problem at a time. He hurried back the way he'd come, straight to the back fence and into the trees.

Jaden hissed at him from the blackness. "Where did you go?"

"I had to get Rainbow's bucket and tie-out rope. We have to hide her."

Sam could feel Jaden's irritation as he headed back to the horse, who was peacefully foraging. He slid the halter onto the mare's head and buckled it on. "I know a place we can tie her out and the people won't find her."

"Okay." Jaden followed. "I think we should stash her, then try to sneak back into your cave for the night. You put food and water in there, didn't you?"

"Yeah, we took everything that wouldn't spoil and hid it in there. How many people are in the house?" Sam led the mare over the bare, stony ground with its bunchy grass toward another buttress of rock.

"There seem to be a lot, at least six. I can tell by their clothes they're people from the plane."

"They won't be mean, will they? I mean, do we have to keep hiding?"

"I don't know. How long will the food in the cave last?"

"But someone will come rescue them soon," Sam said. "Right?" The outcrop of rock was getting closer, but his bad foot was acting up again. He held on to a hank of the mare's mane to take the weight off.

"I don't know, Sam. My dad thinks the explosion could have affected the bigger islands, too, maybe even the Mainland. It could be a long time before anyone comes looking for that plane."

They reached the rock formation. Several scrub guava trees grew around the base, and an underwater spring kept a good-sized patch of grass green even in the summer. Sam tied the twenty-five-foot rope to one of the guava trees. "She still needs water."

"I have a canteen full, and since you've got more in the cave, we can give it to her." Jaden poured the contents of his metal canteen into the bucket. "Let's try to get into the cave."

Back in the grove, the boys worked their way to the tree growing closest to the jutting cliff that sheltered the house from wind and elements.

"Bea put boards from our woodpile over the entrance," Sam whispered. The entrance to the cave was about fifty feet from the back of the house. "We'll have to be really quiet."

Jaden nodded and moved forward. Sam followed—and stepped on a brittle branch. It broke with a crack that sounded like a rifle shot.

They both froze.

"What was that?" they heard from the house. The back screen door creaked as it opened—Sam knew that sound well. They were still invisible in the shadow of the trees. A long moment passed.

"Must have been an animal or something," someone said inside. The screen door creaked again, closing this time.

A few minutes later, Sam and Jaden had all the wood moved aside. Getting the wood back up to cover the doorway was another matter; they were able to balance only a couple of boards back upright.

The cave was so black inside that Sam couldn't see his hand in front of his face.

"I think Bea put a flashlight inside the doorway." The sound of Sam's voice was muffled by the cave walls. He swept his hands along the rock and down. He found the flashlight, a big plastic camping one, and pushed the button. Nothing happened. "Darn." Sam thought hard, trying to remember the layout of the cave. "I think we have a lighter and candles on the shelves."

He felt his way across the blackness until he hit the shelves, began touching and feeling. Everything felt unfamiliar beneath his fingers, just meaningless shapes until he encountered the coffee cans Bea used for seed drying—and then it seemed like his brain switched on and he could tell what he was feeling. Cans of food, the bags they'd hastily brought out from the house, jugs of water, and finally the box of candles, and next to it, the barbeque lighter with its long wand and bulb of fluid.

He pushed the trigger and a finger of flame came out, so bright it stung his eyes after the utter blackness. He lit a candle from the box and handed it to Jaden. They kept the candle going long enough only to locate three sleeping bags, the jug of water, and a couple of granola bars. When Jaden blew it out, the blindfold of darkness dropped over Sam.

"I hope Bea comes back soon." He munched his granola bar in his sleeping bag, his eyes on the faint shape of Jaden sitting in the slit-like doorway, watching.

"I'm sure she will. She'll go carefully and look for us here."

"Okay." Sam took another sip of water from the jug beside him and snuggled down into the padded nylon. He relaxed, exhausted, into a dark so complete that there was no difference with his eyes open or closed. He wasn't even aware of falling asleep.

Bea woke up, a cramp in her leg making her gasp and move, bumping her head on the doorframe of the truck. She'd fallen asleep, and her sore muscles had seized up. She reached down to knead a golf-ball-sized charley horse in her calf.

Bea uncurled herself from her wedged-in position in the seat. "Okay, I better get some energy going to climb back up." Speaking aloud made her feel less alone. She took the water bottle from the bag and unwrapped the crushed malasadas.

Bea closed her eyes to savor the sweet, smooth filling, the chewy dough, the crunch of sugar. Even the smell of the coconut haupia pudding felt like a solid substance, providing energy and comfort. She felt a pang of guilt that Sam wouldn't be able to taste this treat. With that thought, she rewrapped the second malasada, her stomach rumbling in protest.

"Let me see if there's anything we can use in here." Bea opened the glove box and found a universal Leatherman tool, a roadside emergency kit, a first aid box, and a battered flashlight—which didn't work. She stowed the items in her canvas bag and looked in her dad's lunch box. She recognized the food Sam had packed that long-ago morning.

Bea sipped the black coffee from the thermos, draining it, and climbed back out of the truck. It was still deep night, but the moon cast silver light over the steep ascent topped by the dangling rope. Looking up at the rope, Bea could tell she didn't have the upper arm strength to ascend the cliff that way.

Bea worked her way sideways along the rocks at the bottom of the gulch until she found an area where she could climb to the top, coming out well below the steel guardrail that shielded a turn in the precipitous road. She walked barefoot back up to where she'd stashed her things and had tied the rope. She pulled the rope up and untied it, coiling it into her bag.

"Dad must be okay—he got out. Maybe he's home by now." The idea was reassuring—for all Will Whitely's temper and the drinking, he would know what to do next. He was her dad, and his presence was familiar—and in this post-explosion world, familiar was good. Bea swung the gun onto her shoulder along with the canvas bag and set off back up the road with renewed energy, fueled by coffee and sugar.

The house was dark and motionless in the silver light of the moon when Bea finally got there. Still, Bea didn't approach it right away. She didn't see Rainbow in the paddock, and when she snuck up to the porch, she could see unfamiliar backpacks in a jumble on the step.

People were in the house. She wondered if they'd discovered the cave with its cache of food. She needed to check, and somewhere to sleep.

Bea worked her way through the grove to the trees against the cliff and noticed right away that the lumber had been mostly moved away from the opening into the cave. Jaden and Sam must be inside. Bea moved carefully to the opening and lifted one of the boards away.

A hand shot out of the darkness and closed on her wrist. She stifled a scream as Jaden yanked her inside.

"Shh," he hissed, and they both stilled, listening. Bea was much too aware she was pressed against his lean, hard body, and he smelled like smoke and boy. No sounds came from the house—and Bea sidled by him into the absolute blackness, keeping a hand on the wall.

"Where's Sam?" The walls of the cave absorbed sound, giving her voice a muffled quality.

"Probably right in front of you." A flare of flame from the barbeque lighter in Jaden's hand banished the darkness, illuminating Sam's rumpled dark head emerging from a sleeping bag. "You're next to him. I'm by the door."

Bea located her sleeping bag, unzipping it and sliding inside. The light went out and Jaden climbed into his, a rustle of nearness. Bea could tell by Sam's deep, even breathing that her brother was asleep, but now she was keyed up, adrenaline from being startled jangling her nerves.

"What happened with your dad? Did my brothers help?" Jaden whispered.

"I went by myself. The truck was crashed in a gulch on the way to the harbor, and Dad was gone."

"Was he hurt? Where'd he go?"

"I don't know. He was alive, and he got out. I thought he'd be here at home by now."

They lay there in silence.

"Why didn't you get my brothers to help? I didn't want you to go alone," Jaden said.

"I was fine." She didn't want to say how she hadn't wanted to break up their family dinner, how she'd been struck dumb and motionless by the beautiful moment she'd witnessed, by the closeness that Jaden's family had. "How many people are in the house?"

Jaden told her about his reconnaissance and where Rainbow was and Sam's bravery in getting the mare what she needed. "I wouldn't have thought of it," he said. "He knew what to do."

"Sam's a good kid," Bea said. Her hand crept over to touch her little brother's shoulder in the smothering dark. His shoulder blade felt bony as a bird's wing.

"I'm wondering what we should do tomorrow," Jaden said. "We've got supplies here, but they won't last long if the people in the house find out about them."

"I know. We just have to wait and see what we see." Bea's eyes were finally getting heavy. "Thanks for looking out for Sam."

"He's like my brother, too," Jaden said.

Bea felt a stab of disappointment, wondering if he thought of her as a sister, but sleep pulled her down before she could figure out how to ask.

12

SAM AWOKE, FLOATING UP FROM deep sleep into waking. He opened his eyes and realized he could see—light leaked in from the doorway of the cave, and it fell morning-soft across a shape beside him.

Bea.

Her hair was still in the braid from yesterday, curling bits of it escaping around the back of her head. Beyond her, a third sleeping bag with a humped shape blocked the narrow opening—Jaden.

Relief, a feeling like filling up with cool water, rose up in Sam. *Thank you, God, for letting us all get back here safely.*

A cramp in his bad foot and scrapes and bruises competed with the hollowness in his belly. His stomach erupted with a growl, telling him that one granola bar hadn't been enough. Bea rolled over toward him. She was smiling, smoky green eyes sparkling.

"Was that your stomach?"

"Yes."

"Good thing I saved you something." Bea dragged a dirty cloth shopping bag over and reached inside. "It's a little battered, but it will still taste good."

She took out a small, white first aid kit, a black plastic emergency roadside kit, a Leatherman tool, and a pair of gloves. "Here we go." She took out a rounded shape the size of a tennis ball, wrapped in a paper towel. "Bet you can't guess what this is."

Sam narrowed his eyes and sat up. "An apple?" Apples came all the way from the Mainland and were a big treat. Bea shook her head.

"Orange?" Those were even more expensive and special.

"Guess again."

"A dinner roll?" Jaden had sat up in the doorway. "Spam musubi?"

"You wish. Actually, I had a second one, but I ate it last night—got too hungry. One more guess, Sam."

Sam closed his eyes and inhaled. He could smell something sweet, like a doughnut, but it was round. "Malasada?" His sister knew how much he loved the treats the Blue Ginger Restaurant in Lanai City made in its all-purpose kitchen.

"Third time's the charm." Bea handed the sphere to Sam, and he unwrapped the squashed Portuguese pastry. His eyes widened, and he grinned as he bit into it.

"Thanks," he said, his mouth full.

Jaden climbed out of his sleeping bag. He'd taken off his shirt and was wearing just his trunks. He rolled up his sleeping bag.

"Where's the rest of the food?" he asked.

"Shelves. We put all the seeds in the coffee cans so nothing can get at them." Bea sat up. She straightened her clothes self-consciously, smoothing her hair back from her face. Sam wondered what she was worried about. She looked fuzzy and nice like she always did in the morning. "The food's in boxes or cans over there."

Jaden walked over to the shelves and rustled around, opening one of the boxes and taking out a slightly mangled loaf of bread. "We might as well eat the stuff that's going to go bad first."

They made and ate sandwiches of peanut butter and local honey. Sam was still hungry, so Bea gave him a mango. "These are definitely going bad without the fridge."

The three of them clustered in the opening, eating and listening for the people in the house. Jaden had propped the lumber back over the doorway, and Sam felt safe in the cave. Unless the people in the house really went looking, they weren't likely to find them. But there was also a problem with that.

"We're kind of stuck in here." Bea was the one who said what Sam was thinking. "We have to go out. I mean, if just to go to the bathroom."

That had been getting obvious to Sam. He crossed and uncrossed his legs with a need to go.

"I think they're awake in there," Jaden said. "But how do we keep the food and the cave hidden from them?"

"Let's sneak into the trees, then approach the house from the front. After all, it's our house. Say we went looking for our dad and stayed in town overnight, and what are they doing in our house? Play it like that." Bea seemed to be warming to this idea, standing up to brush crumbs off her clothing.

"I doubt they're mean," Sam said. "I think they're scared, just like us."

"We'll have to find out. But what if we can't get back into the cave? Like, they aren't nice and they chase us off, and then we're cut off from our supplies." Jaden's dark brows had a line of worry between them. "I know my family is hoping to come out here if things go bad in town."

"I don't know. That might not be an option. We just have to see how it goes," Bea said. "I still have the rifle, and you have your spear gun. We might be able to drive them off, if we have to."

"But—is that right? I mean, they crashed. They need somewhere to shelter, too," Sam said. He hated to imagine what it would have been like to live through that plane crash and have to try to find food and shelter. How perfect their house must seem!

They might have kept discussing it awhile longer, but noise broke out in the house. Yelling. Scuffles and thumps. A scream. A gunshot rang out from the house, so loud Sam clapped his hands over his ears.

More screams.

Someone burst out the back door, running out into the yard—a young man in a gray hoodie. He looked around frantically and spotted the pile of wood covering the opening to the cave. He ran toward them and dove into the narrow cave opening, landing on his hands and knees. His mouth opened and blue eyes went wide at the sight of them.

Recovering faster than they did, he turned and reached back behind him to move the wood back over the opening he'd made.

"Don't make a sound," he hissed, "or they'll find us."

13

SAM FELT FROZEN. BEA PULLED him into her arms, and Jaden backed up against them so that they huddled together, staring at the intruder and listening to the mayhem in the house. They could hear a loud male voice shouting inside.

"Get out! Or one 'nother one goin' get it!" The voice was harsh—pidgin English marking it as someone from Hawaii.

More thumps. More scuffling. The angle of the house kept them from seeing what was happening, but Sam could tell the movement inside was toward the front of the house. If the people inside were leaving, they wouldn't be able to see them go.

Silence fell.

"What's going on in there?" Jaden whispered. "Who are you?"

The stranger held up a finger to his lips. He turned his head to listen, his ear close to the lumber covering their hiding place. Sam looked around for the old rubber traffic cone he'd found last summer and handed it over. The invader reversed the cone and held it toward the house, the small side to his ear as a makeshift amplifier.

"I can hear them talking inside," the young man whispered. Sam realized he wasn't as old as he'd first seemed—down on his cheeks and a wobble in his voice showed he was still a teenager. "It's a gang. They burst in, were waving guns around, shot my friend Kevin for no reason. Seems like they've kicked my friends from the plane out."

"Oh my God!" Bea's hand covered her mouth. Seeing his sister's alarm, Sam's bladder clenched painfully. "You're from the plane?"

"Yes. My name's Nick. Thanks for letting me hide in here."

Like they'd had a choice.

"Jaden, Bea, and Sam," Jaden said, gesturing to each of them. "I bet it's the LCBoyz. We only have one gang on Lanai."

The LCBoyz were a group of meth heads and small-time burglars whose claim to fame, until now, had been hanging around the low-income housing area wearing red bandannas and a bad attitude. No one took them seriously—but it seemed like it was time to.

Sam needed to pee really bad now. He got up, rummaging around until he found a coffee can without any holes in it. He faced into a corner and used the can, feeling his face flame, embarrassment cramping his bladder so badly he could hardly do what he needed to.

The LCBoyz had a gun. They'd shot someone.

He set the can on the ground and put the lid back on.

"Good idea, Sam," Jaden whispered, giving him a shoulder squeeze. "My turn next. We've been in here awhile," he said to Nick by way of explanation. He stood up and shook out a tarp, stringing it between two shelves as a makeshift curtain. He went behind it for his appointment with the coffee can.

Sam was relieved about the curtain, but it was still embarrassing and the can wasn't going to be enough for long. Clearly they couldn't stay in the cave forever. Nick pretended not to see or hear what they were doing, all his attention on the house.

Someone came out on the back porch. Sam could hear the creak of the screen door. He and Bea craned to see past Nick through a crack in the lumber.

Two young men stood on their back porch, wearing the baggy drop-waisted black jeans and red bandannas the LCBoyz sported. One of them took out a packet of cigarettes, shook one out and tapped it against the railing. He lit the cigarette, took a drag, and exhaled a stream of smoke at the ceiling.

Sam had always hated that smell. Dad used to smoke, before Mom died. She'd gotten on him about it, but it wasn't until she was gone that he'd quit.

"Good thing the guy you shot no stay *make*," the other one said. "We don't need no cops sniffin' around, nailing you for murder."

"Cops are plenty busy in town, too busy to come after us," Smoker said. He was taller and heavier. Older. Tattoos of coiling snakes on his arms seemed to writhe and move as he lifted the cigarette. "We're the ones with guns."

Guns. Not just one gun.

Sam felt like he needed to pee again, but that couldn't be right. He sidled closer to his sister, and Bea draped an arm over him. Jaden moved in close behind them. Nick stayed perfectly still. "What's *make*?" Nick whispered.

"Dead," Jaden said.

"I guess Kevin was only injured, then," Nick said, relief in his voice. Sam saw the older boy's shoulders relax a little. "I can hardly understand their accents."

"Pidgin, it's called," Bea whispered.

"Seems like there should be more food," the younger gang member said, from the porch. "Old man Whitely, he kept his kids out here working. The girl, she brought stuff into town. But there's, like, nothing in the kitchen."

"Where those kids stay?" Smoker said.

Younger did a slow survey of the backyard, and Sam knew what he would see: a metal toolshed. The rocky cliff face, towering fifty feet in the air. Patchy grass they'd barely kept alive in the summer. The grove of trees, butting up against the rocky wall. The pile of lumber they hid behind.

"They had a horse," Younger said. "Maybe they took the food and the horse, hid somewhere. The *haoles* from the airplane said no one was here when they found the house."

"Whatevahs." Smoker stubbed out the cigarette. "This our place now." They went back inside. The screen door slammed a period on the end of that sentence.

Nick turned back to them. "Is this your house?"

"Yes." Bea straightened up, narrowed her eyes at Nick. "And you were trespassing."

Nick put his hands up in a "surrender" gesture. "Six of us came in late at night. We were just looking for help."

"We saw your plane go down," Bea said, and Sam shut his eyes against the terrifying memory. When he looked at Nick, he saw the shadow of that same horror in the older boy's stark blue eyes.

"A group of us went all the way to the top of the island looking for help at Lanai City, and we saw it burning. We knew we weren't getting any help last night, so we came back down here. We knocked and called. No one was there, so we scrounged some food and water and slept in the house. I was up already, trying to make some coffee, when the gang busted in and surprised us. I'm sorry we were in your place, but you've got more serious problems now," Nick said.

Sam crawled over to his sleeping bag and climbed in. They weren't going anywhere, and there was no one who could help them. He turned his back on the older kids, focusing on not crying by pressing his fists hard into his eyes.

"What should we do?" Bea whispered, but he could still hear her just fine. He thought of putting his fingers in his ears—but he wasn't a baby. Shutting it out wouldn't help.

"I don't think we can get past them in the daytime." Jaden sounded apprehensive. "They're on alert for anyone moving around. We'll have to wait until nighttime and then try to sneak by. I think we should go back to town and see if we can find the police and get help. They've shot someone—they're dangerous."

"Don't you think the police will be just looking out for their own families? I mean, do you think anyone's doing the jobs they're supposed to be doing anymore?" Bea asked.

Sam hadn't thought of that and wished his sister hadn't said it. A world where no one was doing what they were supposed to do—everyone just looking out for themselves. This wasn't a world he wanted to know.

"I know this situation is bad, and we're cut off here on Lanai. And I know the LCBoyz are bad news—but our town is a good place where everyone knows one another and cares about one another. Your dad kept you out here by yourselves too long," Jaden said.

"Shut up," Bea flared at Jaden. "Just shut up."

Nick didn't say anything.

Sam could feel Bea and Jaden glaring at each other. Sam pulled the sleeping bag up over his head, put his fingers in his ears, and closed his eyes. He willed himself to sleep. He didn't want to be here anymore, and if that made him a baby, so be it.

Bea stood up and turned away, paced the length of the cave, working off adrenaline from the gunshot followed by discord with Jaden. She hated the feelings that flooded her: anger and fear, intimidation from a stranger in their space. Nick seemed to take up a lot of room, even though she could tell he was doing his best not to offend.

Jaden took the rubber cone from Nick and lifted it to his ear, ignoring both of them. Bea hit the end of the cave and walked back. Six more lengths of the cave, and she felt her pulse coming down, the hot flush of anger in her cheeks cooling. She glanced at her brother in his sleeping bag. He'd pulled the cloth up over his head.

Poor kid. This was a lot for him.

He needs you to be strong. Beosith's voice rang in her mind. *Dig deep. Find your courage.*

Suddenly a picture filled her mind—a group of five of the LCBoyz sitting around the battered coffee table in Bea and Sam's living room, playing cards. One of them was standing, watching out the front window.

Another one was putting together a meal in the kitchen, boiling some rice she'd left in one of the cupboards.

That made seven of them—seven armed and dangerous thugs in her house. Bea did another length of the cave.

"I can't believe there are so many of them." Bea came up behind Nick as he sat in the doorway. "Can you hear them talking?"

"I can only hear a murmur. How do you know there are many? We've only seen two," Jaden said.

"I saw at least five," Nick said. "And there might have been a couple more outside on the porch."

"They're playing cards, getting comfortable." Bea pulled the rubber band out of her braid, combed her long hair nervously with her fingers, feeling Nick and Jaden watching her as she rebraided her hair.

"How do you know?" Jaden angled a sharp, dark glance at her.

"It just makes sense," she said lamely. She sat beside Jaden, wrapping the end of her braid with the rubber band. "I'm sorry for snapping."

"And I'm sorry you didn't get to spend more time in town. It's not fair, how your dad kept you out here."

Bea frowned at Jaden, irritated he was sharing this personal business in front of Nick, a stranger. Nick had resumed his stare out at the house as if he didn't hear them.

"It doesn't matter." Bea's shoulder lightly touched Jaden's. "It's going to be a long day with nothing to do."

"We can't stay here. We have to plan on sneaking out and carrying all the food we can. If we can bring the police back and get those guys out of the house, there might be some way we can keep the food you've got stored. But I think we should organize, pack everything we can carry, and plan to sneak out tonight," Jaden said.

Beosith sent Bea another picture. This time it was Shipwreck Beach, closest to Molokai. The view he sent her was of a washed-up Hobie catamaran without a mast, caught in a pile of debris. *You should go to Molokai. You have family there.* He projected a picture of Bea's aunt, Hilary Hina Kanekoa, with her wide smile and cheeks dented by dimples. *They have the ranch, and Uncle Buzz has his boat. Things would be better for you on Molokai.*

"Aunty Hilary is on Molokai," Bea said aloud. Her aunt was the closest Bea would ever get to her mother, and visceral longing for Aunty Hilary's strong arms filled her.

"Yeah? Molokai's nine rough channel miles away," Jaden said. "Why are you bringing that up?"

"It's a rough passage, but easier than the one to Maui." Even as Bea said it, her throat closed with apprehension. Only the most experienced watermen and women, in the best canoes or boats, ever tried the nine-plus-mile Kalohi Channel between the small islands without an engine. Blasting sideways winds, surging currents, and unpredictable wave patterns made the passage dangerous even in a sturdy boat.

And they didn't have a sturdy boat, or any boat for that matter.

"I was going to Maui to live with my grandparents when our plane crashed. I'd love to get there, but isn't someone going to come looking for us? I mean, does anyone know what this thing was that happened?" Nick asked.

"I heard people in town saying they thought it was something to do with the weird lights in the sky we saw the other night," Jaden said. "Or some sort of electromagnetic pulse bomb. Nobody really knows, but it seems to have knocked out electronics everywhere. Got no idea how much of the islands, or the world even, has been affected."

Bea slapped a mosquito. "We should spend the time we're stuck in here packing all we can and figuring out how we can carry it. But I'm not sure we should go back to town."

"What do you mean?" Jaden asked.

"I think we might do better down at the beach. We can use our fishing and diving stuff, make a fire to cook with. I know where there's an abandoned fishing shack, and we can shelter there. Town looked pretty crazy."

Jaden set his jaw. "I don't care what you guys do. I'm going back to town to bring some supplies to my family and to get the police back out here. You'll see. I'll get these guys kicked out of your house."

"I want to go with you to town," Nick said to Jaden. "I need to find out if anyone can help the other survivors down on the beach."

"Okay. Let's all go together when we leave. We can see what your parents say, Jaden." Bea walked over to the shelves. "Now, let's figure out how to pack this so we can carry it."

Nick watched Bea as she took some supplies down from the shelves. She was tall for a girl, the same height as her friend Jaden at around five foot eight. She had interesting forest-green eyes with flecks of gold in them and curling black lashes. Thick brown hair hung in a braid to her waist, and she wore a dirty athletic tank shirt and worn jeans.

Bea had a kind of wiry slenderness that looked like it came from working hard outside, not dieting and treadmills, like the girls he was used to in the Midwest. He wondered if she was part Hawaiian and that's why her skin was so brown.

"What you looking at?" Jaden hissed.

Nick glanced away. "Nothing."

Nick felt Jaden's resentment and jealousy and focused his attention outside, on the house. Going with these kids seemed like the best way to get help for the crash victims and to find a way to survive for however long it took for this disaster to get resolved. If he was going to be able to stay with these island kids, he was going to have to make friends with Jaden. The last thing he needed was to complicate his life because of a girl.

"So what's life like here, on Lanai?" he said. "When things are normal?"

"Boring," Jaden snapped.

Bea looked up. "I'm sure you'd think it was pretty simple. We spend a lot of time working for food and getting by. What's life like where you're from?"

"Well, its winter right now, so you can bet I was glad to be going to Hawaii," Nick said, with his friendliest smile. "I'm from the Chicago area."

"Why were you coming to Hawaii?" Jaden asked.

Nick shrugged, deciding some self-disclosure might help lower their guard. "My mom died a couple years ago and I was in foster. Finally, my grandparents said they'd take me. They live on Maui."

"Total off-the-plane *haole*," Jaden sneered. Nick frowned. He didn't know what the other boy was saying, but it didn't sound good.

"Jaden! He can't help what happened to him!" Bea said. "That's sad, what you said. And now you can't even get to your grandparents. We're kind of in the same boat—me and Sam's mom died, too, and our dad has disappeared now that the explosion happened. I'm starting to think I'd like to get to Molokai, to our aunt and uncle over there."

"How close is Molokai to Maui?" Nick asked, aware Jaden's jealousy was not abating with Bea's defense of him.

"Same distance there from here. Molokai wouldn't help you get to your grandparents," Bea said.

"Well, I'd like to go with you to town," Nick said, making his appeal to Jaden. "I need to get help for the crash victims, if I can."

"Then let's do it," Jaden said. "And you can get back with your friends."

14

DARK SEEMED TO CREEP ACROSS the straggling back lawn with agonizing slowness. Sam had been awake for some hours now, and his stomach was bulging. They'd eaten the rest of the bread, leftover fish, and other perishables and drank a good deal of water. They weren't going to be able to bring the rest of the perishable food.

The close confines of the cave had begun to feel claustrophobic, but every time Sam went to the opening and heard the mutter of voices, the harsh bad words, the mean laughter—he moved farther back into the cave.

"I think they have a lookout." Bea seemed to know more about the movements of the LCBoyz than she should, but they had nothing else to go on.

"Seems like they found your dad's stash of liquor." Jaden had the cone to his ear. "They'll be passing out anytime now."

So that was why the volume had risen, snatches of song and laughter reaching them. "Maybe they'll all get drunk and we can walk right past," Nick said.

"Still got a lookout, and he's not drinking." Bea put finishing touches on one of their packs. She and Jaden had fashioned makeshift backpacks for each of them out of lengths of rope and cut-up pieces of tarpaulin. Bea had paid special attention to her own pack as she constructed and packed it.

Sam looked inside Bea's. It held rope, another uncut tarpaulin, the roadside kit from Dad's truck, the first aid kit, fishing tackle, and a can of tightly packed seeds, along with all the food she could fit in and her sleeping bag. Bea fastened the pruners and rifle through loops on the outside as a finishing touch.

Sam's pack was more modest—a pouch holding his sleeping bag, slingshot, Dad's Leatherman knife, plus all the granola bars and beef jerky from the shelves. They each had a gallon jug of water to carry.

Jaden's and Nick's packs were the biggest and heaviest, and Bea had given them all the food that had to be cooked—beans, rice, and canned goods. They'd managed to fit most of what was on the shelves into the packs.

"We're going to Jaden's house first, to figure out what to do next from there," Bea told Sam. "Maybe we'll look for Dad."

"Dad didn't come back for us," Sam said. She'd told him that Dad was gone from the truck, tried to make it sound like he must have had to go somewhere else. But Sam knew they were just too much trouble and he'd taken his chance to leave them, after the disaster. "We don't have to listen to him anymore."

"He might need us." Bea's green eyes were dark with worry. He could tell she was feeling weird about Dad. Sam did, too, but his face was finally feeling better, and even with everything that was going on, he didn't miss Dad. He wished he felt guilty about it, but he didn't.

"You guys can bicker over that later," Jaden said. He'd turned his back to them, hoisting up his full pack. "I think it's dark enough. Let's go."

Nick got behind Jaden, his pack already on. He was taller than Jaden by several inches, and wider in the shoulders, too. Sam noticed how hard Nick was trying to get Jaden to like him. He wasn't sure about the older boy, but he did feel sorry for him.

He and Bea pulled on their packs and picked up the gallon jugs of water. Jaden moved the lumber in the opening carefully aside. They could hear laughing and drunken bits of singing. Outside the cave it was full dark, with the moon playing peek-a-boo behind scudding clouds.

Sam moved up close to Nick with his sister behind. He kept his eyes on the ground as they crept forward out of the cave, tiptoeing across the gap between the cave mouth and the first tree. He sighed with relief under the darkness of the trees, but there were new worries here—rustling leaves, brittle snapping branches like the one he'd stepped on that last night.

They moved as slowly and quietly as they could through the trees beside the house. Sam breathed easier as they moved toward the front of the house.

A bellowing bark, way too close, made Sam jump back so that he crashed into Bea. The barking got louder, and he could tell it was one of the wide-chested pit bulls the LCBoyz kept, usually on a big, thick chain. He'd petted those dogs on his rare trips to town and had always thought they were just so the LCBoyz could look meaner.

This pit bull wasn't on a chain. It was barking with a deep snarling sound that made the hair all over his body stand up, and it was getting closer.

Sam turned away and ran.

And he didn't care if he stepped on any branches.

Bea reached out to grab Sam as he broke, fleeing in terror into the darkness, crashing through the leaves—but she missed, and her brother kept going. She slid behind a tree, and the terrible barking didn't get any closer—the dog must have hit the end of its chain.

But now the Boyz were roused, and she heard the stomping of their feet on the porch, yelling and cursing, and the detonating boom of a gunshot.

That's when Bea turned and ran after her brother. She heard Nick, crashing like a rhino through the darkness beside her. The grove, so familiar and sheltering in the daytime, was a black maze. Bea smacked into trees twice, stumbled and went down once before she reached the end of the grove, barking her shin, scraping her hands.

Fleeing ahead of her across the arid moonlit landscape, Sam lurched on, a dark shape. Nick had caught up with him already by the time she cleared the trees. Bea caught up with them and finally glanced back—no one was following.

Maybe they'd just fired the gun into the air. Maybe they were just trying to scare them away.

But where was Jaden?

"Let's get to Rainbow," Sam gasped. He was limping but not slowing down. Bea glanced back again—Jaden still wasn't following.

Bea stopped. Her heart hadn't slowed, because a new fear had taken hold of her.

Jaden shot. Jaden bleeding in the shadows under the trees. Jaden mauled by the pit bull, with its tiny eyes, wide, square head, and heavy jaws. Jaden hauled away by the LCBoyz, trailing blood. Jaden hurt, or dead.

"I have to go back, see where Jaden went," Bea said. "Go ahead. Check on Rainbow and give her water. I'll be right there."

It was a testament to how scared Sam was that he didn't argue, just kept going with that skipping run he used when his leg was bothering him.

Nick dropped his pack and joined her. "I'll come with you."

Bea turned back, calling for the dragon with her mind. *Beosith! I need you!*

The dragon rippled up the slope from the ocean—Bea could see him in her mind's eye. Lanai's geography was simple, open stretches of sun-and-wind-battered red earth scored by dry creek beds from the rare winter floods. Trees were few and far between except on the crown of the island. Beosith came up one of those dry gulches, a faint trail of sparks and the scent of sulfur and fish marking his path.

Find out what's happened to Jaden. Please.

The dragon flowed swiftly past her, the light of his eyes dimmed in stealth mode. She glanced at Nick, to see if he saw the *mo'o* dragon, but the Mainland boy's eyes were on the uneven ground.

Bea slung her pack off and unhooked the .22, leaving the heavy pack on the ground beside Nick's. She cocked the Henry rifle and broke into a jog back the way they'd come, Nick at her side. She could hear the dog from a long way off, and it was still barking.

"What's the plan?" the older boy asked. His voice was calm. He didn't seem as scared as she felt. She could feel heat from his body from their recent exertions.

"Let's just see if we can get back close enough to find out what happened to him," Bea said.

Her mind filled with a picture of Jaden, huddled in the lee of one of the trees near the house. He was holding his ankle, the heavy pack on the ground beside him.

He's all right. But it will be hard to get that close again without them knowing. I will provide a distraction.

What kind of distraction?

Don't worry—I won't show myself. They can't handle *the truth!*

If the situation hadn't been so serious, Bea might have smiled at Beosith's quote from *A Few Good Men*, one of her father's favorite movies. They'd watched it a half-dozen times on the old VCR. Beosith must have watched it, too.

She and Nick stole back into the trees. Even from the far edge of the trees, the dog's barking had a chilling intimidation to it.

"I know this grove. Put your hand on my shoulder and stay close," Bea whispered. Nick did. His hand felt like a clamp on her shoulder, and she shrugged to get him to loosen his grip. They moved as silently as they could through the trees, drawing nearer to the house.

Bea could hear the Boyz yelling and arguing among themselves on the porch. Apparently, some of them wanted to go out and find whoever had been in the grove, while others in the gang thought they should stay guarding the house. They didn't mention Jaden, so Bea knew they hadn't found him yet.

"Shut up!" someone yelled at the dog, which had renewed its barking as they approached. The pit bull sounded like Cerberus—the three-headed dog that guarded the entrance to hell—but that was probably just the dark and her overactive imagination. They finally reached a tree close to the house, and the lights of candles and lantern illuminated the Boyz on the porch and the dog chained to the corner of the house.

Suddenly, the barking turned to panicked yelping—and Bea spotted the dog running away, its intimidating bellow changed to cries of terror as it fled into the dark, chain flapping.

"Catch the dog!" she heard someone shout. Several of the Boyz boiled off the porch, lurching after the animal in pursuit, while others called directions, waving their guns. Bea wished she could find it funny—but the guns prevented that.

You're welcome, Beosith said. *I think I broke a tooth on that chain.*

"Bea!" She'd almost stepped on Jaden. "You shouldn't have come back."

"I couldn't leave you here—what happened?"

"Twisted my ankle. I can't run, especially with the pack."

In answer, Nick had already pulled the other boy to his feet and looped an arm under his shoulder. With Jaden

121

hopping, they disappeared into the darkness under the trees.

Bea heaved Jaden's pack on. It was really heavy, and the rope straps dug into her shoulders. The grove seemed to go on forever, the yelling and drama at the house fading behind them. Once out of the grove, they were able to move a little faster. When they got to the backpacks, Nick stopped.

"I can carry a pack. We shouldn't leave anything." Jaden lifted Bea's pack and put it on. Nick put his back on, too, and lifted Jaden again. The boys semi-hopped and hurried as best they could over the uneven ground.

Bea had a stitch in her side by then, breath tearing through her lungs. She used the rifle as a walking stick, eyes on the moonlit ground interspersed with tussocks of dry grass, trying to keep from tripping.

She almost walked right into Rainbow. The mare pushed Bea in the chest with her nose in greeting. Bea hugged the mare around the neck, the warmth of the horse's scent instantly soothing her.

"I thought we could put the packs on her or something," Sam said. "You okay, Jaden?" He'd led the horse by her halter and put the riding blanket back on.

"Twisted ankle," Jaden said. "Your sister saved me." His thankful words infused her with warmth.

"Nick was the one to get you out of there," Bea couldn't help pointing out. "Good thinking bringing Rainbow here, Sam." Bea rubbed the mare's forehead in greeting. "Let's put Jaden up on her with the packs."

"Sweet," Jaden said. "Now you're talking."

Bea directed Nick to make a stirrup with his hands. Jaden put his good foot in it, grasping the horse's mane.

He swung his hurt leg over Rainbow's back with a stifled moan. Once he was settled, Bea handed up the heaviest packs and Jaden stacked them in front of him. Nick donned Bea's lighter one.

"Let's get moving. Some of the Boyz wanted to come looking for whoever was out in the trees," Bea said. "Catching that dog won't take them forever."

Jaden, Sam, and Nick didn't need any more urging to get moving. Bea wished she could tell the boys about Beosith's bold move in scaring the dog, but the words stuck in her throat. How would they ever believe her?

Bea sensed the dragon out on the broad plain, chasing the terrorized dog back toward the Whitelys' house and enjoying every minute of it.

Don't have too much fun, Bea thought. *Meet us at the Apucans.*

The mare broke into a trot, and the three of them hurried across the barren field, headed uphill toward Lanai City.

Nick's eyes seemed to have adjusted by the time they reached Lanai City, and he was stumbling less on the uneven ground. Periodically he scanned the vault of dark sky for the light phenomena Bea had described from the night before, possibly presaging the event that had happened, but the sky was empty of anything but moonlight and starshine.

Sam apparently had a limp, and now he was up riding behind Jaden, his arms around the older boy's pack and waist. Bea walked beside the mare, the rifle in one hand and the horse's rope in the other.

They reached the top of the ridge that looked down at Lanai City. The tiny town seemed to have quieted from the scary glimpses he'd seen through flames. They headed down the road. Cook fires flickered in the yards of unburned houses. Off on the right as they passed into the town, half of the Lanai Lodge and its banyan trees were blackened rubble. The main Lodge area still stood, though, and from a distance, Nick could see the moving shadows of people around a bonfire in the middle of the turnaround.

"I bet that's where the airplane people end up," Bea said. "All those folks are off-islanders; they'll get together."

"They won't have any food," Sam said, worried.

"Yeah, but they have money," Jaden said. "And people will help them."

"What good is money now?" Bea said. She shot a quick glance at Jaden. "I mean, with the ferries not running, or planes or anything."

Nick kept quiet, conscious of the heavy money belt around his waist. He looked at the Lodge. "Maybe I should go up there. See if that's where my friends ended up."

"No," Bea said decisively. The uneven light flickered in her large green eyes. "I met a guy there. Tried to steal Rainbow. I don't think you should go alone. Come with us to Jaden's house first, and maybe we'll go up there tomorrow and take some food to the people there. Right, Jaden?"

Nick glanced at the dark-haired boy atop the horse. Jaden gave a single sharp nod. Nick could tell that now that he'd helped the other boy, Jaden felt obligated to offer hospitality—but he knew if Bea hadn't spoken up, he'd be hiking alone up to that fire-lit building.

Looking over at the hotel, Nick thought about the other kids he'd been with until he took shelter in the cave. They'd probably had to keep looking for food, water, shelter, and first aid. They were probably up there at the hotel. The beach didn't have anything to offer them or the other plane survivors, not even fresh water.

The disaster, whatever it was, had struck so suddenly. Nick, along with everyone else on the plane and all people on this tiny island, had each been minding their own business, each circling in their own orbit—when suddenly, everything changed. Those left were just lucky to be alive.

Now the challenge was staying that way.

This place didn't seem like it produced a lot of its own food and water. He felt a little guilty for the half loaf of bread he'd stuffed into his stomach before he left the cave—and he dismissed the feeling. The bread might have to last him a while, and it would have gone bad.

"Maybe if everyone got together, they could chase off the LCBoyz." Sam was still talking about the gang who'd invaded his family's house.

"We're going to the police with that," Jaden said. "Nothing but guns can stop guns."

"If the police are still doing their jobs," Bea said.

"Even if there aren't many police, I know Lanai City," Jaden said stoutly. "Most people aren't at all like the LCBoyz. They want to help one another. We'll be trading rather than using money if people stop believing in it. And the hotel guests and airplane people can work for their food, too. They'll be fine."

Nick kept his mouth shut. He hoped Jaden was right.

They arrived at what appeared to be a small cottage, set close to the street with lamps in the windows. Bea tied the horse to the porch rail, and a short woman with long, silver-streaked hair in a bun and a tropical-print dress threw the door open with a cry. "Jaden!"

Nick stood aside, feeling awkward, as people swarmed out of the little house. Jaden's mother kissed and hugged Jaden after several other kids had helped him get off the horse—clearly he had a big family. Nick wondered if they were Mexican, realizing he'd never met anyone that looked quite like them in the Midwest.

Sam was embraced and clucked over by Jaden's mother and a couple of other girls, while Bea went to Nick's side and took his arm. She tugged him over to a square, sturdy older man standing in the light falling from the porch.

"This is Nick. He escaped from the crashed plane, and he's been helping us."

"I'm Matteo Apucan." He shook Nick's hand. "Jaden's father."

Jaden joined them in front of the porch. "My mom, Jiselda. These are my brothers, Joseph and Jeremy. My sisters, Jasmine and Jenna."

Everyone eyed Nick. The older sister, Jasmine, had a flirty smile and long, shiny black hair. He'd never felt so white and awkward in his life. "Glad to meet you all. Does anyone know what happened?"

"Let's go inside," Mr. Apucan said. "We can sort out everyone's stories there." The backpacks were unloaded and taken inside. Nick saw Bea lead the horse around the back of the house. Mrs. Apucan exclaimed happily over the contents of the backpacks. Clearly, food was already an issue.

The family ranged around several couches in a small living room with a dead TV in the corner. Nick sat down, and the little girl, Jenna, plastered herself against him.

"You're so tall," she said admiringly. Nick couldn't help smiling.

"Jenna!" her older sister frowned. "Give the guy some room to breathe! Sorry, Nick. We don't get too many *haole* Mainlanders in our living room."

"That what I am?" Nick lifted his brows in surprise. "What's *haole*?"

"Caucasian. White person," Jenna said. "Mainlander is from, like, anywhere not in Hawaii."

"And what are you?"

"Filipino, and proud." Jaden was the one to answer that one, and Nick didn't think he was imagining the hard note in the other boy's voice. Once Bea had returned, Jaden got his father's attention.

"We need to call the police."

"What's going on, besides the disaster?" Mr. Apucan asked.

"The LCBoyz took over the Whitelys' house. They ran off the airplane survivors who were squatting there and shot one of them. They scared us off, too." Jaden told the story of what had been going on with contributions from Nick as Bea wedged herself onto the couch between Jaden and Jenna.

"Well, I have some bad news there. We had only three police officers on duty here on island when the solar event happened, and they aren't enough to keep peace and order without backup. So we're helping them. We're working with our Neighborhood Watch to walk the streets and keep people from looting and such. We wondered where the Boyz went."

"They seem to be making our house their headquarters," Bea said. "They have guns."

"Joseph," Mr. Apucan called over to a teenager who looked younger than Jaden. "Go get Police Chief Roberts."

"Sure, Papa." The teen trotted out, puffed with pride at his errand. Meanwhile, Jasmine propped up Jaden's ankle and wrapped it in an Ace bandage.

"Too bad we don't have any ice," she said. "We have some aspirin, though."

"I'll take some," Jaden said. "So, Papa. Like Nick asked—does anybody know what the explosion was? Why it knocked everything out?"

"We think it was a solar storm, an electromagnetic pulse wave sent out by the sun flaring up. We were hearing about the special effects in the sky on the radio before it went down. Doc Padilla thinks it's an electromagnetic pulse burst—the sun sort of had a hiccup, he says."

Jaden turned to Nick and Bea. "Doc Padilla worked for the University of Hawaii. He's a retired astronomer and lives over here."

"How bad was it? How far does the damage go?" Bea asked. "Is it just on Lanai? It seems like it must be bigger. The pulse brought down that plane on Keomoku Beach."

"We don't know, but we assume it's affecting at least all of Hawaii. So far we haven't had anyone contact us—not that we have any working equipment they could contact us with. We haven't seen any planes. The only communications from the outside have been a few sailboats over from Molokai. So—where's your father?" Mr. Apucan asked Bea.

"He went off the road in his truck during the event. I found it, and it was empty. He—we don't know where he is."

Mr. and Mrs. Apucan exchanged a long glance, and Nick saw her nod before Mr. Apucan said, "You can stay with us as long as you like."

Nick wondered if he was included in the invitation. Mrs. Apucan's eyes had gone to the pile of food they'd brought on the counter, and a little line appeared between her brows.

"We're not sure what we're going to do, but thanks for taking us in tonight," Bea said, and she looked right at Nick when she said it. Nick felt his chest constrict with a strong emotion—gratitude and something more. Bea had taken him in like a brother, but the feeling he was beginning to have about her wasn't brotherly. *She's brave, strong, kind, and pretty.* He'd never met a girl like her, and she was treating him like he mattered.

That hadn't happened often.

Jeremy, who looked around Sam's age, tugged on Sam's arm. "Want to come see my comics? I heard you like comics."

"Sure." Sam slid off the bench to follow his new friend.

"You kids need to go to bed in the next half hour," Mr. Apucan said. "We have to save the lamp oil and candles."

That gave them time to get organized in bedrooms. Mrs. Apucan was putting Sam in the boys' room and Bea in the girls' room. "We don't have enough futons," she said, frowning, as Nick helped pull linens out of a tiny closet. "You'll have to sleep on the couch in the living room."

"That's fine, Mrs. Apucan. Thanks so much." Nick followed her, carrying a load of linens, and helped make up the extra beds. Then she covered one of the couches with a sheet and handed him a hand-sewn quilt.

It wasn't long before the small three-bedroom cottage, full to the brim with people, was settling into sleep. Nick, comfortable on his couch, felt himself fully relax for the first time since he'd gotten on the plane days ago on his journey to Hawaii.

15

BEA WOKE UP BEFORE DAWN in the girls' room. Her sleeping bag on a futon on the floor had been comfortable, and she'd slept with the total blackness of the exhausted. Beside her was a bunk bed containing seventeen-year-old Jasmine, and Jenna, aged eleven, Jeremy's twin. Sam slept in the boys' room on the bottom of two bunks housing Jaden, Jeremy, and Joseph, and she knew Nick was in the living room.

Bea looked up at the old-fashioned lath-and-plaster ceiling, which muffled the drum of rain on the tin roof. It would not have been fun to be trapped in the cave, or even down on the beach in that leaky fishing shack, while a summer downpour soaked the thirsty island and snuffed out the last of the fires.

It felt strange to be so surrounded and absorbed by the family. She wasn't sure how she felt about it. But she was clean, her belly was full, and for the first time in months, she felt safe.

Guilt followed that realization. Her dad was missing, and in spite of the disaster, she felt safer in the Apucans' house than she had at home. It made her realize that, disaster or not, things had reached a breaking point with Dad.

Jasmine had told her last night that the first thing the Apucans had done when the town's water system failed after the disaster was build a rooftop catchment system. Bea could hear water rolling off the tin roof into gutters, siphoning through a screen into big plastic barrels around the house.

The rain couldn't have come at a better time. She wondered about the plane people—according to Mr. Apucan, they'd ended up at the Lodge with the other hotel guests—but the townspeople were helping them, bringing up all the food and water that they could spare on a rotating basis. Plans were being made to convert the hotel grounds to food gardens, but everything took time, and they were all still hoping for some sort of rescue.

Lanai City wasn't the lawless free-for-all Bea had feared. Her dad had been wrong about the town, and she wondered what else he'd been wrong about. She closed her eyes, remembering the talk with the police chief at the Apucans' dining room table after the younger children had gone to bed.

"We don't have the manpower to get the LCBoyz out of your house." Chief Roberts's uniform was filthy, streaked with mud and soot. He'd taken his hat off, and thinning brown hair was plastered to his head. "Some of the Neighborhood Watch people, like Mr. Apucan here, are now deputies. Our priorities are keeping order, keeping the looting down, getting first aid to people hurt in the disaster or the aftermath. Frankly, we're glad the Boyz are out of town, but I'm sorry that it was your house they moved into."

Bea had folded her lips tight and shot a glance at Nick, who was frowning. "They shot someone from the plane," Bea said. "They have guns."

"All the more reason that we have to leave them alone for the moment." Chief Roberts turned red-rimmed, tired eyes to her. "We have only a few firearms, and our first aid responders are totally overwhelmed. The last thing we need right now is a firefight with the Boyz. If they start coming into town, harassing people, we'll deal with them." He took a sip of water from a glass Mrs. Apucan handed him. "I'm sorry it's not better news, but it's good to know where they're located. You kids have been through a lot—and I've added your father's name to the list of the missing."

"Are there many people missing?" Bea asked.

"Unfortunately, yes. We've lost people in the fires and in vehicle accidents. Some of the boats in the harbor burned, too." He must have seen something in Bea's face, because he squeezed her shoulder. "If he wasn't in the truck, he made it out alive and he's somewhere on the island—unless he took a boat to Maui or Molokai."

Bea perked up. "Boats are going there?"

"Yeah. There have been a few taking people back and forth. For a fee, or trade."

"I need to get to Maui. I was on my way to meet my grandparents there," Nick said.

"Well, we haven't had any boats from there yet. I suspect things are in pretty bad shape over on Maui—so many more people in trouble."

133

A long pause as they all considered the situation on Lanai, magnified a hundredfold on the bigger island with a population of a hundred and fifty thousand, plus another several hundred thousand visitors. Bea suppressed a little shiver and glanced over at Nick. He was looking down at his hands. His face looked tense, and his eyes were opaque as blue china.

"What's happening in the rest of the world?" Jaden asked.

"We don't know much. Other than a few boats getting in from Molokai who were planning to come anyway, we haven't heard anything. Molokai was hit much like we were. Without any electricity, communications are completely down, and we're really worried about how far the damage goes. It's not a good sign we haven't had any planes or been able to communicate with Maui." Roberts stood, set his hat on his head. "I'll let you know if I hear anything about your father," he said to Bea. Turning to Nick, he said, "I advise you to sit tight until we know more about what's happening on Maui. You could be going from the frying pan into the fire over there."

"Thanks," Nick said. Bea wanted to pat his shoulder, but she saw Jaden frowning at her, like he was jealous or something. Mr. Apucan walked Roberts to the door, talking with the captain about his shift on the Watch, as they were calling the group of civilian deputies that were on duty each day.

"It seems like the Boyz are going to get away with taking over our house," Bea said.

"Just for now," Jaden had said to her as they'd headed to bed. "See? It's not as bad as you thought it was going to be. People are pulling together."

Jaden had been right on some things, and Bea was right on others. For now, here in a comfortable bed, with protection and food, was the right place to be. She wriggled a bit on the futon, turning over in her sleeping bag. She wondered where Beosith was.

Right here. The dragon sent her a mental picture of the inside of the Apucans' garage, a structure used as a workshop and storage area. Beosith was curled on a pile of full chicken-feed bags. *It's a good thing they have all this— they can cook this corn for people to eat.*

Bea unzipped her sleeping bag. She wore a clean pair of sweatpants and a fitted, scoop-necked T-shirt that belonged to Jasmine and fit just right, along with the bigger bra that she'd hoped for. She tiptoed through the house, glancing over at the dim humped shape of Nick and making sure he hadn't moved. She went to the side door leading to the garage, unlocked the door, and tiptoed down the wooden steps.

Hey, buddy. I've missed you. She sat on the feed bags beside the dragon, who'd curled into a coiled ball. Beosith cracked his eyelids, emitting a faint glow. He had a slightly musty smell she'd always liked. She scratched between his brow ridges, and his scales lifted and fluttered with pleasure. "I'm so glad you're still with me."

I'll be here as long as you need me.

"So why do you think we should go to Molokai?"

Your family is there.

"The Apucans are treating us like family. And Dad can come find us here."

Your family *is there.*

The slight emphasis on "family" made her frown. "Did Dad go over there?"

No answer from the dragon.

"We're tired of running around. We'll see what happens tomorrow." She stood up. "I want to go up to the hotel and check out the situation with the plane people."

Hide the horse.

"You got that right. I'm not letting anyone take her away." Last night she'd turned Rainbow loose in the Apucans' fenced backyard. Bea opened the door into the backyard to check on the mare.

Morning was lightening the rain-dark sky, but she could see the mare standing in a lean-to with a couple of the Apucans' milk goats.

"She's fine. I better get back in the house." But when Bea turned back, Beosith was gone. She could see why—Nick's rumpled head looked out the door, blue eyes blinking sleepily at her.

"What are you doing up?"

"Just making sure Rainbow's okay." Bea crossed her arms over her chest self-consciously, chilly from the damp of rain. Nick came down the steps. He had on a pair of loose nylon gym shorts and a thin tank shirt he must have borrowed from Jaden. He scrubbed his hands across his face and ran them through his short, spiky blond hair.

He was so different from anyone from the island. So much taller, with ivory skin over smooth, long muscles and those blue eyes. She wished she didn't find him attractive. Nothing could come of it, she told herself firmly. He was on his way somewhere else, and he'd never fit in here in a million years. He was probably longing to be back in the big city—though what if the disaster had gone as far as the Mainland?

There was no telling how the world had changed.

"Rainbow's probably enjoying being with the goats. I saw them last night."

Bea looked back out. Sure enough, several nanny goats were pressed up against the mare, making the most of her warm side as rain trickled off the roof of the lean-to. "Seems pretty cozy."

Nick had come to stand beside her in the doorway. She felt heat from his body.

"Hope you were cozy, too, last night." His voice was almost a whisper.

Something was prickling into awareness between them. Bea wondered what the side of his neck smelled like, the curve just between his ear and shoulder. She had an impulse to find out and turned her head just a little. She breathed in the warmth of his hair, freshly washed last night in water heated on the stove. It smelled even better than she'd imagined, a little like watermelon shampoo with a warm note that could only be him.

Nick turned, too. Their faces were almost touching. She could feel him looking at her, and she kept her eyes down, shy. That meant Bea was looking at Nick's beautiful, defined mouth, his lips tucked in at the corners as if keeping secrets. His mouth seemed to tell her something about who he was, this mysterious stranger fallen from the sky.

She suddenly thought of Jaden's mouth. She'd been thinking about it a lot and wondering when they'd kiss. Jaden had full lips with a curl at the corners like he was on the verge of smiling. She knew him so well, and until today Jaden had been all she'd ever wanted.

Now all Bea would have to do to kiss Nick was to tilt her head up just a little—she could feel him waiting to see if she would. Her heart pounded so loud she wondered if he could hear it. She eased away and headed for the door into the kitchen. "Do you want to go up to the Lodge to see if any of your friends ended up there?"

"Definitely."

Nick followed Bea into the kitchen. They ate some mangoes and starfruit from a bowl on the table as the rest of the house woke up. Mrs. Apucan approved of their plan, filling a shopping bag with items they'd brought from the cave—beans, rice, and local sweet potatoes. "We can spare these to share with the people up there."

Jaden had joined them. "I want to see how the plane people are doing, too."

Glancing at him, Bea felt guilty she'd even thought about kissing Nick. She'd barely known the Mainland boy for a day, and Jaden had been her special friend for years! She felt her cheeks get hot. She pretended she'd dropped something and bent down to hide her face.

"You kids going to the reef anytime soon? We could sure use some more fish," Mrs. Apucan said, looking at the depleted food storage cupboard. The worried line was back between her brows.

"Sure, we can do that," Bea said, thinking of the fishing shack near the end of Shipwreck Beach. It might still be a viable idea for her and Sam to go camp there. "Thanks for sparing some things for the people up at the Lodge."

"Of course. We're all in this together," Mrs. Apucan said. Bea felt bad, remembering the negative things her dad used to say about the family. Her father had been jealous of Mr. Apucan's success at his job when the Apucans were nothing but generous.

Bea, Nick, and Jaden set off through town, carrying Mr. Apucan's huge striped golf umbrella. The rain had decided to come down hard again, and the bags of food were heavy as they splashed through town. Bea felt something shiver through her again as her shoulders brushed the boys' under the shared space, but she kept her eyes on the ground, avoiding debris and rubble, her rubber slippers quickly becoming slippery.

Jaden had put on rubber boots and pointed to her now-muddy feet, black with ash and dirt. "Pretty."

"Brat." She elbowed him. "You could have found me and Nick some boots."

"Jasmine took hers. She'd gone to the neighbors' for something. And my dad was using his," Jaden said. He sped up. Bea had to trot to keep them all under the circle of the streaming umbrella.

They eventually made their way up the long, slanted drive to the remains of the Lodge. Bea frowned at the smell of the blackened banyan trees—a sharp stench like wet, burned hair. Jaden led them up under the large portico, and Bea shook the umbrella out, leaning it against the huge double doors, stuffing down the apprehension that tightened her chest.

Nick scanned the people camped out in clusters all through the room. It was furnished in a classic "lodge" style, with antler chandeliers and rock fireplaces. The seating area's couches had been made into beds. Groups had staked out areas defined by thick woven carpets, little islands on a sea of hardwood floor. The far side of the Lodge was a bank of paned windows; today the window looked out at pouring rain, a row of pots, buckets, and barrels catching the water streaming off the roof.

"Nick!" Ashley had spotted him and ran across the room to hug him. He let her, feeling awkward, glancing at Bea and Jaden. "We thought something happened to you!"

"It kind of did. But what about Kevin? Is he okay?"

Ashley's blond hair was straggling with damp, her jeans and T-shirt filthy. "He's hanging in there. There's a nurse from the town who's been coming up and doing first aid for us here. We're all so glad it's raining."

"Us too," Jaden said, from beside Nick. "Are you from the plane that went down on the reef?"

"Yeah." The girl cocked her head, pushed her hair out of her face, examining Jaden with curiosity.

"I hid in a cave behind the house where we spent the night, and Bea and Jaden and her brother, Sam, were there. It's their house," Nick said.

"Oh, we didn't mean to break in," Ashley said to Bea, biting her lip. "We just needed a place to sleep."

"Don't worry about it," Bea said. "But we do want to get the gang guys out of the house as soon as we can. Did everyone make it up here to the Lodge?"

"Everyone who could make it came here." There was a note of finality in Ashley's statement. "No one's left alive on the beach, if that's what you're asking."

Bea's mouth opened and closed, and her face paled. Jaden took her hand.

"Bea and Sam saw your plane go down," Jaden said. "It must have been terrible."

Nick felt a frown tighten his brows. This was the first time Jaden had showed any concern about the crash at all, and now he was holding Bea's hand.

"Come meet some people. I'm Ashley—but call me Ash," the blond girl said.

"Jaden. And this is Bea."

Ash led them around other groups. People turned to look at them curiously, but no one interfered as Ash led them to a large group against the wall.

"Nick!" Zune spotted him and scrambled up. His dreads were even more matted than before. Nick endured more hugs and backslaps. He introduced Bea and Jaden around. It felt strange to have this many people glad to see him.

Kevin was lying on a row of couch cushions on the floor. His shoulder was bandaged with what looked like torn, bloodstained sheets. He was pale, with patches of red on his cheeks. Nick approached and squatted beside the blond surfer. "Damn, Kev."

"They didn't even give me a chance. Just shot me right on the couch," Kevin said. Bea had come close and knelt beside Nick. She pushed forward the canvas bag of food and handed it to Ash.

"We had some food put by. This is for you. I'm sorry I never met you at the house." Jaden and Nick added their food bags to Bea's.

"Wish you'd come home instead of the gang," Ash said.

"They'd have chased us off, too. In fact, that's what they did." Bea told how they'd been hiding in the cave all day until they were able to sneak away

Nick looked up as a big, beefy, red-faced man elbowed his way through the group to join them. He wore a soiled lavender golf shirt, and he scooped up two of the food bags. Another large man took the last one. None of Nick's fellow passengers said a word.

"Hey!" Nick exclaimed.

"We're in charge of food distribution," the man said. His eyes narrowed in recognition of Bea. He pointed at her. "You're not welcome here. This girl is a looter."

Bea stood up. "Not true. Who put you in charge?"

"Everyone living here at the Lodge."

Bea looked around at the group of airplane survivors, and none of them would meet her eye. She yelped as Golf Shirt grabbed her elbow, hauling her toward the door. Nick heard the man hiss in Bea's ear, "Bring me that gun and that horse, or I'll come take them from you."

Nick scrambled after them as Golf Shirt frog-marched Bea across the lobby. He grabbed at the man's arm, but his companion, a burly black man, pushed Nick away so hard he staggered.

"Hey!" Jaden yelled, but both boys were cast aside as the men dragged Bea, struggling, across the crowded lobby.

"Let her go!" Nick yelled. "She didn't do anything but bring you some food!"

The two men ignored their protests, and suddenly all three of them were shoved out the front doors of the Lodge. The tall double doors slammed behind them. They heard the *thunk* of something slotting through the big brass handles at the back.

Bea was shaking, Nick could see, but she hid it by looking around for the umbrella, which had disappeared—someone had taken it. Jaden put his hands on her shoulders and turned her toward him. "You okay? What did he say to you?"

"He wants my gun and Rainbow," she said. "He saw them when I was here looking for Dad." She blinked to hide tears, rubbing her arm where the man had grabbed it. Jaden hugged her, and Nick felt a twinge, wishing he could be the one to comfort her.

"That guy's a jerk. He can't take anything from you." Jaden was flushed with anger under his tan, dark eyes flashing. "I'll tell Chief Roberts about him."

"So much for me staying here." Nick had donned his own clothes before they came to the Lodge in preparation. "I thought I'd stay up here with my friends from the plane, but that dude doesn't seem to want any of us here."

Jaden frowned. "You'd be better off here. With your own people."

Bea pulled away and frowned at Jaden. "His people? Jerks like that guy who threw us out?"

"I meant Mainlanders. *Haoles*. People like him. You know what I mean," Jaden snapped, apparently surprised Bea didn't agree with him. Nick knew exactly what the other boy meant. He didn't belong with the Apucans, and he knew it—he was the wrong color, to start with.

"No worries. I'll find another way into the Lodge." Nick adjusted his belt and felt the comforting heft of it. He might have lost his backpack at Bea's house, but he still had his take, and money still had to have some value.

"I never took you for such a redneck," Bea said to Jaden. She turned to Nick. "I'm sorry my friend is prejudiced. He must have forgotten I'm half white, too."

"No! That's not what I meant!" Jaden exclaimed. "I just meant—you know. Outsiders belong up here at the Lodge."

"Shut up," Bea said. "You're just digging yourself deeper. But that's fine. It's your house, and your family gets to say who stays there. Nick, you can find the fishing shack on Shipwreck Beach if you can't get back in with your friends. Just follow the road to the end and you can't miss it." She looked stiff and angry, green eyes sparkling and mouth tight, hair that had escaped the braid curling around her face.

"I appreciate that, but I'm sure I'll be fine," Nick said as confidently as he could.

Bea stuck out a hand to shake his goodbye.

"A little formal, don't you think?" Nick drew her gently into his arms. He shut his eyes so as not to see Jaden's furious expression and to fully experience how good she felt. The top of her head just brushed his lips, smelling like the watermelon shampoo they'd both used last night. Her arms enclosed him, and he felt her supple length against him for a precious moment.

"Bye," Nick whispered into her hair.

Bea let go abruptly. She turned and set off at a fast walk into the rain, which had slowed to a patter. Jaden gave one last glare and trotted after her.

Bea glanced at the blackened banyan stumps, all that remained of the magnificent trees that had shaded the Lodge, with a frown.

"Those trees will grow back before you know it, my dad says." Jaden followed her gaze. "Banyans are like weeds, super hard to kill. Dad and the crews were always having to deal with the keiki trees popping up all over the grounds."

Bea could tell he was trying to smooth her over. She just walked faster. There was no sense discussing the situation with Nick further; Jaden had those attitudes and, if Bea were honest, if she hadn't liked Nick so much she'd have thought the same thing.

"Your mom wanted us to go fishing. Let's go down to Shipwreck Beach." When she'd calmed down, Bea finally gave voice to her odd sense of urgency to get down there. The broken Hobie cat was never far from her thoughts.

"We can check it out. But I don't think you and Sam should be down there by yourself."

Bea folded her lips tight. He'd just try to argue if she said she wanted to stay there. She didn't like how jealous he was acting with Nick. Not that she liked Nick or anything. She just felt bad for him. She glanced back at the Lodge. Shrouded by rain, barricaded shut and surrounded by burned trees, it looked like something out of the zombie apocalypse—and she realized they'd had the apocalypse, all right. Next came the zombies.

Sam didn't want to go down to the beach. His lower lip went out as he scowled at his sister. "It's raining."

"So what. You won't melt."

"Why do I need to come? You and Jaden catch all the fish, anyway."

"I want you to come, because…" Words failed Bea as they entered the house. She didn't want to tip her hand that she wasn't planning to come back. Mrs. Apucan was peeling taro at the sink. Sam's new friend Jeremy came to stand beside him, lending backup.

"I don't want to go with you," Sam repeated.

"I thought you wanted to go fishing with us."

"Well, I changed my mind."

Bea saw Sam was limping worse than usual as he got up from the table to head down the hall. His leg must be hurting from yesterday's escape from the cave. Jaden's ankle was much better, but then, he was still wearing an Ace bandage.

"Oh, let him stay," Mrs. Apucan said, from the sink. "He can help Jeremy weed the garden."

Jeremy gave a theatrical moan. "It's raining, Mama!"

"Well, when it stops. You boys should be doing chores since we don't have school."

"Okay, then. We'll do our best to get something for dinner." Bea let the screen door bang behind her as she went to the backyard to fetch Rainbow. Jaden followed.

Bea didn't say a word all the way down the path to Shipwreck, which was mercifully empty of people. Jaden, riding double behind her, got the hint and kept quiet, too.

She kept thinking of their family on Molokai as the horse moved down the trail toward the beach, and she gazed at the bigger island just nine wind-whipped ocean miles away. Her uncle Buzz had always made her feel so safe, and safe was something she longed for. She'd grabbed the .22 and slung it across her back with a carry strap, and having it close made her feel a little better.

At the beach, Bea took her pry tool, opihi bag, and spear out of their hiding place under the log. She sat down and pulled her reef tabis on, heading straight out onto the windswept reef, rough with afternoon surf and not the ideal time for fishing.

Her nerves were still rattled from the encounter with Golf Shirt in the Lodge, and she was too distracted to be able to spot fish at first, but eventually became absorbed in the hunt as it cast its spell over her. She moved over the reef and scanned the deep tide pools, and her roiling emotions calmed, the activity focusing her mind. She speared a fat silver *nenue*, scooped it flapping into the air, and turned to where she'd left Jaden. He was way off down the reef, standing perfectly still in knee-deep waves.

The throw net, a ten-foot circle of hand-woven fishing line netting trimmed in flat bar weights, was draped carefully off Jaden's shoulder, hip, and right hand. Hung with precision, it was ready to fly open and drop in a circle over a school of fish when he threw it. She noticed the alert line of his gaze into the receding waves as he waited for just the right moment.

Bea brought the *nenue* in and shook it off the spear's tines into the bag to join a couple of round purplish sea urchins she'd added—they made a good soup if properly prepared. She glanced back, just in time to see Jaden throw the net with a powerful gesture perfected by hundreds of hours of practice. As it was meant to, the net spiraled out into its full diameter, reminding her for a second of a ballet dancer's skirt. It dropped into the waves, disappearing, and Jaden leaped in after it, catching hold of a colored cord attached to the center and hauling it back in. The net came alive with flapping manini, a green striped tang that was delicious pan-fried with butter and garlic. Her mouth watered at the thought.

Bea followed Jaden in as he carried the laden net to the beach. They both knelt in the sand to harvest the fish and had collected a good-sized pile when they'd untangled them all. Jaden whipped out his knife and began cleaning them. Bea got to work with the ease of practice on her fish, some of them still flapping. She inserted the point of the knife between the pelvic fins beneath the gills, holding the fish flat against a rock as she cut, facing away from herself, to the vent near the tail. Using a finger, she hooked out the guts and tossed them into a tide pool.

She wrinkled her nose. Manini guts always smelled particularly strong from a diet of algae and reef growth.

"Think that's enough for today," Jaden said. "We'll need another bag for more." He rinsed the fish in the water, packing them neatly into his fish bag.

"Okay. I want to check out the plane wreck. See if there's anything useful left behind there."

"Excellent." His eyes flared wide with excitement. He'd been withdrawn since the Apucans' house, and she could tell he was relieved she'd shaken off the encounter at the Lodge.

"How's your ankle?" Bea asked, glancing at him as they walked through the sand toward the horse. She carried the loaded bags and Jaden his heavy net.

"Sore." Jaden now wore a neoprene brace his parents had given him. He stowed the net in his backpack. They hid their equipment under the beach log and mounted Rainbow with the fish bags tied together and dangling on either side of the mare. Bea guided the horse up onto the rutted dirt road that ran along the beach most of the way around the island and headed toward Keomoku, the long beach facing Maui where the plane wreck lay.

Ash, the girl at the Lodge, had implied that everyone who could move up to the Lodge had done so. Bea's heart beat with heavy thuds. What did that mean? Would they find people dying, too injured to move? Would there be bodies everywhere? "Move it, girl."

Jaden tightened his arms around her waist, his breath fluttering the hair at her ear as he said, "What's the hurry?"

"Just want to get this over with." She noticed the way his arms felt around her, both warm and strong. "I want to see if there's anyone we can still help and if there's anything good we can salvage."

"We should have thought of that earlier," Jaden said. "But I guess it was good we got the fish first. They need the food at home." Bea wondered if he still had to hold her quite this close, but she didn't say anything as the mare moved into a gentle canter and ate up the couple of miles around the coast to the wreck site.

Rainbow came to a halt on her own at what was, to her, a familiar grazing spot in front of the kids' favorite swimming hole as Bea and Jaden stared, unspeaking, at the wrecked plane.

Waves had come up in the intervening days since the plane had gone down, pushing it further in toward shore. Mostly intact, it still had a terrible look about it, like a dead seagull with a torn-off wing. They slid off the mare without speaking. Rainbow had already dropped her head to graze.

Bea looped her reins around a tall naupaka bush, scanning the area.

The beach was deserted.

A makeshift shelter filled with airline pillows and blankets marked where the survivors had camped. A mountain of opened suitcases, spewing clothing and useless items like hair dryers and electric razors, formed a mound that the teens walked carefully around.

Bea looked down the beach and drew in a sharp breath as she pointed. "Look, Jaden."

A row of six driftwood crosses, high above the tide line, marched like forlorn, drunken soldiers down the beach. The empty camp was a testament to suffering and loss, and its atmosphere of misery seemed to seep into her very skin.

She didn't want to be there long. "Let's take a look at the wreck and go."

Jaden nodded in agreement. They walked down through the sand and waded waist-deep into the pool. Detritus from the plane littered the water—broken seat belts, plastic breathing masks, disintegrating magazines, even the squat shape of an unopened carry-on rested on the bottom of the pool near the open door of the plane.

The door opening into the wreck beckoned.

Jaden reached up into the rubber-lined aperture and hauled himself into the aircraft with a heave of his arms. He squatted on the ceiling that was now a floor and offered her a hand. Bea shook her head and boosted herself in on her own with just a kick into the water below. They moved in to explore the interior.

The seats ran upside down all along what had become the roof to the tail of the plane. Seat belts dangled. There was a smell of brine, mold, and the sweetish stench of something rotten. The overhead compartments that they stood on had opened and coils of released air masks waited to trip them. Bea turned toward the cockpit and moved forward to investigate.

The plastic of the plane's ceiling was slick and slippery, as if it were covered with condensation or the beginning of algae, and the door of the cockpit was open, revealing that the small windows in the front had been blown inward, and the sea now filled the nose of the plane. Dead instruments, fogged with water, rose above the water coming in. The pilot's seats were mercifully empty, but Bea guessed that the pilots had at least been injured but more likely were feeding crabs on the beach right now.

Her stomach lurched as a small wave splashed her.

"There's nothing useful here." Bea moved backward and bumped into Jaden. The space felt claustrophobic, the smells overwhelming. "Let's get out of here." She squeezed past him and jumped down into the pool, splashing rapidly across to the shore. She turned back. Jaden was still in the plane.

16

NICK TURNED BACK TOWARD THE forbidding-looking Lodge. Clearly going back in the front door wouldn't work, but there had to be a side exit open. He could just sneak back and join his friends. He was good at getting through a crowd without being noticed.

On that thought, he put his hoodie up over his already-soaked head and broke into a trot through the wet grass around the outside of the hotel. He passed the back doors with their lineup of catchment containers and went on along the brick walkway toward the breezeway that had connected the main lodge area with the section making up rooms.

The breezeway had been hacked through to keep the fire in the rooms section from spreading, and Nick spotted a side door next to the breezeway's splintered infrastructure. He leaned on the push bar, but the door was locked.

The rain was coming down harder, soaking his clothes, and he really wanted to get inside now. He reached up into the opening that had been hacked into the breezeway and hoisted himself inside, careful of the splintered wood and blackened ash.

The roof remained on the breezeway, and there were about six feet of covered area before another door with a push bar that led inside. He pushed on the brass bar gently and quietly, easing it open just an inch, so he could orient himself to the interior.

It was dim inside, the only illumination coming from the windows and the heavy cloud cover cutting that natural light down considerably. Fortunately, the door into the breezeway was separated from the main lobby by a foyer-like room with restrooms on either side of it. Nick could hear the murmur of voices inside, but there was no one in the foyer.

He eased inside and then, hoodie well up over his head and back hunched in a universal don't-look-at-me teen posture, he slouched into the main room, drifting along among the groups as if headed somewhere slowly but definitely. And he was headed somewhere.

Nick entered the group of young people around Kevin with smooth grace, materializing alongside Zune.

"Hey," he said in a low voice.

"Dude!" Zune exclaimed, and everyone spotted Nick now.

"Keep it quiet, please. I don't want to get thrown out again," Nick whispered, and his friends clustered close but kept their voices down. Ash snuggled against his side, patting his sweatshirt.

"You're all wet."

"I know. So who is that jerk in the purple shirt?"

"Name's Kent. Says he owns stock in this hotel so that makes him part owner. And yeah, he's an a-hole," Ash said.

"He seems to be running things okay, though," Zune said. "He organized different teams to do stuff. We have cleaning and kitchen duty every other day, and there's a group foraging on the grounds and in the village for food."

"So he wasn't just stealing the food?"

"No. We pool everything, and the team on KP cooks the meal. We all eat, and we all get a portion."

As if agreeing with this idea, Nick's stomach rumbled. "When is the next meal?"

"You don't need to know." Nick recognized Kent's voice just a second too late to make a break for it as the big golf-shirted man and his burly sidekick grabbed him by the arms and hoisted him up.

"Hey, Kent. This is our friend! He helped us get off the plane!" Ash cried, grabbing for Nick. "He's a good guy!"

"We don't have food for the people we have, let alone a kid who got here with locals. He can find somewhere else to scrounge a meal."

"Let go of me!" Nick snarled, struggling. Instead, the men dragged him to the front door and, once again, he was humiliatingly ejected.

His arms were sore and his cheeks hot with humiliation as he picked himself up off the steps, feeling the familiar gut-ache of rejection.

He stood, pulled his hoodie back up, and walked down the steps and out into the gracious turnaround driveway, trying to calm his ragged breathing and jagged emotions. A few hundred yards away from the building, he paused under the dripping branches of a pine tree lining the driveway to consider his options.

He could go back into town and look for shelter with the Apucans. Something told him that, though the parents might be okay with him crashing, Jaden would find a way to make him regret it.

He could try to find someone else to shelter him in the town.

Or he could go down to the beach and look for the fishing shack Bea had told him about. She was planning to go there, and maybe that was a way to see her again.

Besides, he'd had about all the company of other people he could take.

Making up his mind, Nick went over to a nearby trash barrel and looked around inside for anything useful. Finding a couple of quart-sized water bottles, he jogged back to the building and filled them at one of the downspouts.

Unfortunately, there was nothing to eat in the trash can, but maybe he could catch something at the beach. His stomach growled loudly, casting a vote.

He wished he had his backpack, but it was back at Bea and Sam's house with the gangsters. Inside he'd had a lighter, a big packet of beef jerky, a spool of potentially useful duct tape, a couple changes of clothes, and the small bedroll sleeping bag he'd never been without since he went into foster care.

Putting his head down so the rain didn't hit him in the eyes, he headed up the road out of town.

Bea got herself under control, looking across the miles of blue-water channel to Molokai. She missed her aunt with a sudden visceral longing. She could almost feel Aunty Hilary's strong arms around her, hear the slightly husky alto voice: "When you goin' stop growing, girl?"

Her aunt always smelled of Monoi Tiare coconut oil, which she used to keep her supple brown skin beautiful. She was the closest person physically to Angel Whitely that Bea might ever see again, and just thinking of her aunt made Bea's eyes prickle with all the tears she kept inside behind that wall.

Their Uncle Buzz was dear, too, a gruff, barrel-chested fisherman who never, for a moment, made her feel anything but loved. They usually went to Molokai for several weeks in the summer, taking the ferry over and shoehorning in with their cousins—but they hadn't gone this year. Dad had said he couldn't spare them from the chores, but Bea knew he was afraid they'd want to stay with the Kanekoas.

Aunty and Uncle had their own children, their cousins Keala and Aukai—but Bea and Sam knew they had a special place in the Kanekoa home. Maybe the boat idea wasn't so crazy. Maybe they were supposed to get over there, and if Beosith thought they could make it—maybe they should try. Her `aumakua hadn't steered her wrong so far.

She turned back to the mountain of luggage. The survivors had probably taken all that was useful out of it, but maybe there was something there that could help with the boat.

Jaden eventually joined her as she rifled through the mountain of duffel bags, suitcases, and golf club sets. He held a brace of sturdy webbing up. "I cut off these seat belts.

They seem useful. And look at this." He held out a compass, an apple-sized plastic orb floating in liquid. "I found this in the cockpit. I think they brought this in separately. It attaches with a suction cup." He showed her how the orb swung in a little frame with the suction cup on the bottom.

"Cool." Bea gestured to a small pile she'd begun. "Some of these clothes could work for your family. I've got another pocket knife, and check out this rope." She showed him a coil of tightly woven rope and a packet of pitons. "Someone must have been planning to do some climbing."

They were energized by these useful discoveries, and Bea squelched down a feeling of guilt as she dug through a suitcase of women's clothing, selecting anything that could fit the Apucan girls.

This was salvage, not stealing—and the plane people would have taken anything they could use already.

Ready to return, Bea sat on the horse and settled the bundle of salvage on top of her thighs as Jaden slung the fish bags on either side of the mare. Suddenly, Rainbow snorted, lifting her head in alert.

"Hey!" they heard, followed by a familiar bellowing bark that shot a jolt of adrenaline straight to Bea's heart.

The pit bull.

The LCBoyz must be coming to check out the wreck, and now Jaden and Bea had been found.

Beosith! She thought frantically.

The dragon sent her a picture of a deep ocean cave, fish scattering before him. *I'll come as fast as I can.*

He was nowhere nearby.

Jaden tried to climb up behind Bea, but she had her hands full as the mare half reared, neighing.

"Grab on, Jaden!" she cried, as she struggled to hold the horse in while fighting her own terror—the dog was coming for them, a brindled missile running down the beach. Jaden leaped up, wrapping both arms around her waist in a desperate grab, and Bea clapped her heels against the horse's sides. "Yah!"

The mare bolted down the hard track. Bea felt her belly tighten, her shoulder blades tingling as she bent low, terrified of a gunshot. She clutched Rainbow's mane as the mare hurtled down the road, accelerating to a full gallop. The salvage items formed a hard ball Bea wrapped herself around, hunkering down close to the horse's neck.

She could feel Jaden's panicked struggle to stay on the horse as he bounced around behind her. The only thing he really had ahold of was her waist, but she felt his arms tighten as he pulled himself up and settled his legs behind hers on the riding blanket.

The fish bags bounced against the horse's sides and Bea wished she could take the time to drop them, lighten the load for the mare, who continued a frantic pace, turning to follow their familiar trail uphill.

Bea could hear the dog barking. It was still following.

Jaden tugged at the rifle slung across her back, one of his arms still banded around her. "Give me the gun."

Bea straightened up, unslinging the rifle. The mare was tiring, gusts of breath heaving through her, blowing heavily. Her head pumped with the effort of packing two while running uphill on the rugged trail, and sweat darkened her neck and shoulders.

Jaden levered the rifle to cock it, and Bea felt him turning, one arm still around her waist. She glanced back down the trail, and the dog was still following—it had stopped barking and its tongue hung out, but it was still after them, pig eyes gleaming.

Jaden tightened the rifle against his side, swiveled awkwardly around, and Bea heard the *crack* of the modest report.

"Dammit. I missed." He aimed again. "This won't kill him, but maybe it'll make him stop following us."

"Do it!" Bea said, as Rainbow dropped into a trot. The mare was close to giving out.

Crack!

This time, when Bea turned to glance back, she saw the pit bull's hindquarters retreating downhill.

Sam hobbled out of the house as fast as he could when he saw Bea and Jaden walking back on either side of the sweat-darkened horse.

The day of chores and togetherness with the Apucans had begun to wear thin, and he was surprised at how happy he was to see his sister's face, pink across the nose and cheeks from a day at the beach—even overcast and rainy as it had been.

"What did you get?" he asked, as he took the bulging bags they handed him, lifting them off the horse.

"We got chased by the LCBoyz," Jaden said. "Other than that, a good fish score on the reef, and we salvaged some stuff from the plane wreck."

"Oh my God," Mrs. Apucan said, coming out on the porch and wiping her hands on a dishtowel. "You kids okay?"

"Thanks to Bea's rifle, yeah," Jaden said, nodding to the .22 slung over Bea's shoulder. He lifted the fish bags off the horse while Jeremy grabbed Jaden's heavy backpack. "Let's get the fish sorted and we'll tell you all about it."

"We should rinse the net," his younger brother Jeremy said.

"Can you do it?" Jaden asked. "I'll do the fish." He headed for the garage sink while Jeremy carried the net to one of the rain barrels that had a tap at the bottom.

The Apucans dispersed as smoothly as a well-oiled machine, leaving Bea and Sam alone with the duffel of salvaged items she'd gathered at the crash site. She led Rainbow, head hanging, into the backyard, gesturing for Sam. She looked around, apparently checking that they were alone.

Bea's brows were drawn together over her green eyes. A few freckles that appeared with the sun had broken through her tan, and her thick, unruly hair was barely contained by the braid. She knelt and unzipped the duffel bag, showing him various items. "I want us to think about getting a boat together and going to Molokai. I want to get to our family over there. They have the ranch, and there's more food, and they can protect us if things get worse."

"That's crazy," Sam said automatically. He squatted with her, their heads close together over the bag. "Why are you telling me this?"

"I don't feel safe here." Their eyes locked, and Sam thought of all the challenges they'd been through, from the Boyz taking over their house to the man at the Lodge.

"The Apucans will look out for us."

"I know they'll try, but we're taking up food and space. I can tell it's going to be a strain on them. I don't want us to be a burden. We should be with our own family."

Sam frowned. He'd seen Mrs. Apucan's worried looks, too. "Where would we get a boat?"

His heart had begun a series of heavy thuds as he thought of the windy, surging, deep channel between the islands. On the other hand, being with the Apucans had reminded him how great it was to be with Aunty, Uncle, and their cousins on Molokai—and he'd been thinking of them on and off all day. But what if they were having problems from the disaster, too?

There was just no way to know.

"There's a wrecked Hobie cat washed up at the end of Shipwreck. I think we can rig it up to sail, be over there in just a few hours."

"What're you guys talking about?" Jeremy inserted himself, his wide white grin inviting secrets. "Did you find any more comic books in the luggage off the plane?"

"You're so lucky. I did." Bea dug in the bottom of the duffel and produced a couple of Spider-Man comics. She handed one to Jeremy and one to Sam. "We go tomorrow morning, Sam," she said, command in her voice, as she found a clean rag to rub Rainbow down with.

17

WHEN NICK FINALLY REACHED THE beach, it was nearly dark. His clothes, damp from the rain that had stopped on the other side of the cup of ridge that held the town, chafed his legs and kept him damp, so that even though it was warm, he shivered in the chill generated by a breeze blowing up the side of the island off the sea. Eventually, he took off his hoodie and jeans, slinging them over his shoulders and making his way down a path off the main road toward a beach he could clearly see.

He spotted the rusting hulk of a shipwrecked cargo vessel embedded in the reef. It seemed so close from above, and yet, by the time he was at the beach, he was stumbling with hunger and tiredness.

No one was around, thankfully, to see him walking along the dirt road above the beach, fish-belly-white legs gleaming in the dusk, boxers flapping, everything he owned in the world draped over his shoulder.

It seemed like he'd walked forever when he finally spotted a dark structure that must be the fishing shack tucked under some tallish bushes. He fumbled his way inside.

There wasn't much to recommend it. The floor was sandy dirt, and he could feel a couple of splintery built-in bunk beds with no mattresses. There was another open door that faced the ocean, and a roof.

That was all.

Feeling in the dark, he hung his damp clothing from the edge of the top bunk and went out through the front opening.

The moon lit a path bright as crumpled tinfoil across the black ocean. Reflections danced off tiny lapping waves. A nearby palm tree's leaves rustled, and the sand looked like molten silver in the moonlight. This beach would be paradise on some other night, when he had a full belly and was warm, but now his body was racked with shivers. His stomach had gone from rumbling protests to a constant ball of aching.

Nick sat in the sand looking at the ocean and sipped some water just to give his stomach something to work on. How could he catch fish with nothing to even make a hook and line out of? In the dark?

Maybe he could trap some in a tide pool or something.

But then how to cook them?

No. He was just going to have to go to sleep hungry.

At least he was too tired to care too much. With one last look at the mockingly pretty beach, Nick went back into the shack and lay down on the hard wooden bunk.

Morning seemed to take forever to come. Nick woke a hundred times during the night to strange noises: squeaks and rustles in the long grass nearby, the unfamiliar shushing of surf and clattering of palm fronds. The pinch of hunger pangs and the jab of splinters from the bare wooden bunk alternated with waves of goose bumps rippling across his body as the night breeze blew over his chilled skin.

Finally it was light enough for him to see a hand in front of his face. He needed to find some way to catch fish, and he was ready to eat whatever he caught raw.

Nick found a stick under the trees and a couple of rocks and spent a half an hour or so sharpening a point onto the stick. When it was sharp enough to hurt when he poked himself, he set off onto the reef. He left his shoes on, since they were still dirty and wet from the day before and he didn't want to poke his feet on coral or sea urchins.

An hour later, the sun was finally really up and Nick had done nothing but throw his makeshift spear at a few tiny fish that skittered away easily.

He was beginning to feel light-headed when he went back in to the beach. He had to find something better than the stick. Maybe he could find some discarded fishing line and some way to make a hook.

As he trekked back toward the shack, he spotted the twin plastic hulls of a faded Hobie cat protruding from a big pile of driftwood and debris.

Perhaps he could clear the debris off and get to Maui on it.

Almost immediately the impossibility of such an idea hit him. There was no mast or sail, not to mention he didn't have a clue how to sail or even where Maui was. Still, he poked around in the debris pile, pulling the piled-up wood off the hulls. Along the way he found a scrap of net.

He could use the net to trap fish. Nick untangled the net from the driftwood it was wrapped around and took his stick and went back onto the reef. He looked carefully until he found a deep tide pool with a smaller one attached. He strung the net across the opening of the smaller tide pool with room for fish to swim under it.

Then he jumped into the waist-deep, bigger pool and, using the stick, tried to scare the fish hiding around the edges into the small pool.

He saw a few dart in, but by the time he reached the net to lower it to the bottom and trap them, they'd darted back out.

He peppered the air with curses and whacked the water in frustration. The sun was high by then. His back, as white as his legs, had begun to fry in earnest when he finally admitted defeat and went back to the shack.

He would have cried if he'd had enough water left in his body to cry.

He drank half the water bottle, looking back up the steep arid hump of the island in worry about what to do when the second bottle was gone. It was going to be a long, ugly walk back up to the village, where at least there was water and the possibility of food. He'd have to wait until nightfall when it was cooler.

He stretched out on the bunk to sleep. There was nothing more he could do, and his body was simply giving out.

Bea shook Sam's shoulder and he woke groggily. There was a crease in his cheek from the crumpled Spider-Man comic he'd fallen asleep on. "Come on, Sam," she whispered.

Sam crawled out of the sleeping bag and rolled it up in the pale-gray predawn, hurrying. She saw him tuck the comic in with Jeremy. They sneaked out of the bedroom filled with the soft breathing of sleeping boys.

In the kitchen, Bea filled water containers. "Take whatever food you can fit into your pack," she said. "I brought a lot of fish in yesterday. That'll pay for what we take."

She watched Sam fill his backpack with the granola bars that they'd brought from their cave, beef jerky, bags of nuts and raisins, and three oranges. Her mouth watered at the sight of the oranges and the thought of their citrusy deliciousness breaking open in her mouth.

Bea put her finger over her lips for quiet, and they stuffed his tightly rolled sleeping bag into the pack and hoisted it up. They sneaked out of the house, and Bea led Rainbow out of the backyard, causing a chorus of protesting bleats from the goats.

Bea mounted and gave Sam a hand up behind her. As they approached the table rock outside of town, Bea pulled the mare up.

"Just a sec. Got to leave Jaden a message." She slid down and clambered up to the slit in the rock and stuck a bit of paper, folded into a diamond, into it.

Bea felt all her doubts come back. They'd just sneaked out of the Apucans' house, repaying the kind family with an unexplained departure and a raid on their nonperishable food supplies. Sam scooted back onto Rainbow's rump so

Bea could mount up, and this time she nudged the mare into a trot.

The words she'd written on the note were burned into her mind.

Don't come after me. We are going to Molokai to our family there. Thank you for all you and your family did for us, but we have to get to our own family. Don't worry. We'll be fine. I'm letting the horse go after this, and I want you to find her. You know the places she likes to go. I will miss you.

She'd ended the note without a signature. It was what they did in case anyone found their notes. It had been hard not to even draw a heart, hard not to tell Jaden what they were doing, but she knew he'd want to come if she did, and she couldn't do that to the Apucans.

Saying goodbye wasn't something she knew how to do very well, anyway. Never had learned how. Just thinking of saying goodbye to her horse made her legs tighten, and Rainbow picked up her pace to a gentle canter. Sam's arms tightened around her, and they crested the road out of the cup of mesa where Lanai City was held as if in the palm of a hand.

From that ridge, the magnificent view opened with the morning-lit panorama of red-gold Molokai dead ahead, a mere nine wind-whipped ocean miles away.

Don't worry. I'll be with you every inch of the way, Beosith said. She hadn't heard from him yesterday except for the dog chase and realized she hadn't missed him—the day's dramas had been so all-consuming.

"That boat better be there," she muttered to the *mo'o* dragon, picturing the Hobie cat wreck he'd been sending her pictures of.

It is. I wouldn't lie to you.

"What?" Sam asked, his chin grazing her shoulder. Her little brother was almost her height, and it was still a little surprising.

"Nothing. We have to find something; then we can settle into the fishing shack."

Rainbow took them down their favorite well-worn goat track to Shipwreck, and they continued along the rutted red dirt frontage road to where it ended at a huge pair of boulders and became a fisherman's trail.

Keep going, Beosith said, so they rode the mare between the stones and along the trail to the far end of the beach. Around a jutting cliff, another beach began. In the corner of the farthest end of the beach was a huge tangle of washed-up driftwood, tangled plastic bottles, coral-covered scraps of old fishing nets—and protruding from the detritus, the faded twin hulls of an old Hobie cat.

"See?" Bea slid off Rainbow to land in the sand. "We do have a boat." She felt a wild burst of energy and excitement. They weren't stuck here, kids without a home. They really could get to Molokai. Beosith would make sure they got there safely.

"I don't know, Bea." Sam dismounted behind her. They took off their heavy packs and set them in the sand. "I don't know."

"You'll see. We'll have to do some work, but I just know this is how we are going to get to Molokai to stay with Aunty and Uncle." She approached the wreck. It was nearly buried in jumbo-sized driftwood and other trash. "Good thing all this junk was covering this up, or someone else

169

would have taken it by now." She spotted signs of activity around the wreck. "We got here just in time."

Bea pulled the driftwood off the buried hull. She and Sam worked together, lifting and hauling away broken branches, tangled piles of washed-up netting, various types of plastic trash, even a small plastic wading pool, until the boat was uncovered. In less than an hour they had it cleared, then stopped for a snack and water break. Chewing a piece of beef jerky, Bea eyed the remains of the Hobie.

It had been orange at one time, and now the tops of the twin hulls had faded to peach. The trampoline was completely gone, but the aluminum frame connecting the hulls was intact. The mast was gone, and so were the rudders, and one of the hulls had a hole in it. She watched a crab scuttle out of the fist-sized hole.

She had no idea what to do next.

Bea had sailed on a tourist catamaran out of the main harbor once on a whale watch, so she knew how this kind of craft could skim through the water with little resistance and not a lot of sail even—but how to rebuild the craft?

And with what? Just fixing the hole in the hull was beyond what they had in their backpacks. She didn't even remember what a catamaran looked like rigged up, let alone how to sail one.

She took a sip of water. "What now, Beosith?" she whispered.

No answer from the dragon, but Sam held up a bleach bottle. "I think I can cut a piece of this out, and if we have some glue, or resin, we can fix that hole."

"Okay. Maybe we'll have to go back to town." She kept forgetting what a knack Sam had for fixing things.

"Yeah. I think we can make a rudder out of these, maybe."
He held up a couple of squares of storm-battered plywood.
"But we're going to need nails. Some wire. Don't know how
we're going to get those things we need. No stores are open
obviously." Sam had begun to assemble a pile of potentially
useful items.

"I have wire." Bea opened her backpack, took out the
spool she'd taken from the cave, and added it to the pile. "If
you know what you need, I can find it."

"Hinges. More rope. A long pole for the rudder. Clamps.
A windsurfer sail, with a boom and mast," Sam muttered. "A
couple of life preservers…"

"A windsurfer sail?" Bea perked up. "I remember seeing
one at the end of Kaiolohia Beach; must have washed in
from Maui. Let me take Rainbow and go look. I can also try
to find the rest of what you need."

Bea hauled herself onto Rainbow and trotted away,
happy to have something she could do. They'd passed the
fishing shack on her way out, but drawing adjacent to it
now, she decided to stop and take a look inside, see if it was
as habitable as she remembered.

Bea backtracked to the fishing shack, built of silvery
unpainted scrap lumber. The simple shelter was set back
from the beach under a naupaka tree, the common beach
shrub that often grew large enough to cast shade. Bea tied
Rainbow out near a patch of grass, gave her some water in
an old paint bucket she found at the shack, and went inside.

She sucked in her breath in a gasp. "Nick!"

The older boy was lying on the hard boards of one of
the built-in wooden bunks nailed to the wall. Nick startled
awake at her voice and lifted bleary blue eyes. His pale skin

was burned a deep crimson across his face, shoulders, and back, and he wasn't wearing anything but a pair of black boxers. "Bea!"

He scrambled to sit up, and she turned her back, blushing, but not before she'd seen a lot of his long, muscular body. "I'm sorry to wake you up."

"Thank God you did." She heard the rustling of him pulling on the jeans she'd spotted hanging off the upper bunk and slipping into the black T-shirt with Chicago Bulls on it. He joined her in the doorway, pushing his hair back and combing it with his fingers. "Please tell me you've got some food."

"Yes, but ...we need to save it for something." She felt bad saying it. She could see how hungry he was by his hollow eyes, and he tightened his belt around his narrow hips.

He looked down, threading the belt through a loop. "I understand."

"No, it's fine. Let me go get something for you to eat from our backpacks; then Sam and I can go fishing and we'll make a real meal." She led him outside and pulled up Rainbow's reins. "You might as well know what we're doing." She hopped up on the mare and extended a hand to him. "You can pack on behind me."

"I've never ridden a horse before." Nick's cheeks had gone even redder, this time with embarrassment.

"You scared?" She guided the horse up next to a rock. "Just sling a leg over and put your arms around my waist."

Nick got up on the rock and, one hand on her shoulder, slung a leg over Rainbow and settled behind her tentatively. She could tell he was trying not to crowd her, but as

Rainbow moved out with a snort at the extra weight, he tipped backward and had to grab her, pulling in close.

Bea pretended indifference to the feeling of his jeans-clad thighs against the backs of her bare legs, his long arms tight around her waist as he clutched for balance. His cheekbone bumped the top of her head. He was so different from Jaden, who was closer to her size and familiar.

"We're just a short way up here." Her voice came out breathless. "I was going to look for a windsurf sail. We're going to get this Hobie cat ready to travel."

"I saw that," Nick said. She felt him rest his cheek against her hair as he relaxed into the rhythm of Rainbow's stride, settling his body around hers. "This isn't so bad. Horseback riding."

"Maybe we should try a trot."

"No," he said so quickly that she laughed.

Just then they came around the corner to see the Hobie cat, uncovered, and her brother taking a break with the backpacks under one of the naupaka bushes.

Sam scrambled to his feet. "You found Nick!"

"He was sleeping in the fishing shack."

"And he's hungry," Nick chimed in. Sam laughed and opened one of the backpacks.

"Just give him a granola bar and an orange to tide him over," Bea said. "We need to go get some fish so we don't use up our supplies."

"Sounds good. Oh, man. I'm looking forward to one of those oranges, too," Sam said.

"We deserve a treat after all that hard work," Bea agreed.

They clustered in the shade of the naupaka tree, sitting in the sand, and Sam handed them each an orange and Nick got a granola bar. Bea pretended not to hear the loud growl of Nick's stomach as he wolfed down the food.

Her own belly was just as loud as she peeled the orange, inhaling the citrusy scent as she broke off each bit of peel. She and Sam ate their oranges slowly, letting each juicy bite melt in their mouths. Nick, already done with his, hung his hands between his knees, looking out at the ocean.

"Don't know when we'll ever have another one of those," Bea said, and handed her last slice of orange to Nick.

"I'm not used to thinking of them as a big treat," Nick said. This time he shut his eyes, savoring the bite of orange. "But everything is different now."

"Yes, it is. I think we're going to keep finding out how different," Bea said. The three of them looked over at the boat, revealed in all its battered potential.

"Think we should try to hide it?" Sam asked.

"No. Too much work." Bea's exertions seemed to be catching up with her. She yawned.

"We have a lot more work to do, and we need some stuff to do it," Sam said, frowning.

Bea went still and put a hand on Nick's arm to caution him. He froze as he spotted what she'd seen. One of the small, sand-colored francolin quail, brought over to Lanai for hunting fifty years ago, scratched in the leaves under a nearby naupaka.

Beside her, Sam slid his slingshot out from his back pocket, loaded a lead weight, and pulled the thong back, tracking the bird as it scratched and moved into the open. He sighted and let fly.

The plump little quail never even chirped. It burst into the air in an explosion of feathers, falling dead to the ground. Sam hurried over and picked up the limp bird.

"Now we have to get the fire going. These aren't very good raw."

"Awesome!" Nick exclaimed. "You have to show me how to do that."

Sam grinned. He flipped open the Leatherman he carried and hacked the bird's head off. He hung it upside down to drain. Blood pattered on the sand, and the air filled with a coppery smell. Bea smiled at the way Nick watched in fascination.

"Nice shot, Sam," she said. "A few fish ought to round things out."

"I tried for hours and didn't get anything. You guys have to show me how it's done," Nick said.

"Well, it helps to have the right equipment. We have to go get it. Our fishing gear is hidden over by the shack."

They walked back to the shack, leading Rainbow. Bea tied her out and made sure her bucket had water. Sam put on the extra pair of tabis Jaden had left behind under their hiding log and took out the pry tool, the three-prong spears, a couple of masks, and a handheld line and hook, which he handed Nick.

"You can use this," Sam told Nick. "We just need a shrimp for bait."

He showed Nick how to catch one of the small transparent opae shrimp by grabbing a cluster of limu on the side of the tide pool and trapping the opae in the leaves. Bea pulled her clothes off over her head, uncovering the bathing suit she wore underneath. She pulled on her tabis and sharpened the prongs of her spear between a pair of stones.

"Follow me," she told Nick. "I'll take you to a deeper pool where you can catch something bigger."

Sam took off in another direction across the reef as Bea led Nick through knee-deep water. "Tide's kind of high, but that's good in some ways. The water's deeper, and the fish are moving around, looking for food. You okay in those jeans?" She slanted a look back at him.

"They're fine." Nick was clearly having a hard time pushing through the deeper water behind her and was creating a lot of turbulence. She stopped him with a hand.

"No splashing. Just glide along. Like this." She demonstrated a smooth stride that kept the water undisturbed. "I'm glad you have shoes on. There are a lot of ways you can pierce a foot, and it'll get infected."

He followed her slowly until she reached the large pool where she'd caught the eel a few days ago—days that now seemed like years in how much the world had changed.

"Find a spot where you're out of view. The fish can see you up above the water, you know." She touched his arm, positioning him so his shadow fell away from the pool. "Now, let out the line and jig it up and down gently above the bottom so the shrimp seems to be moving." She demonstrated, then handed him the ball of line wrapped around the stick. "You do it."

She got him situated, then said, "I'm going diving. Sam's just over there, so give a shout if something goes wrong."

"Can't imagine what that would be, beginning with how do I get a fish off the hook if I get one," Nick said ruefully.

Bea grinned. "You'll figure it out, city boy." She swizzled a little water in her mask, spat into it, swirled the mixture around, put it on, and slipped under the water, spear in hand.

Nick watched Bea's sleek figure sink beneath the waves in the shallow water. He couldn't keep his eyes off her as she swam away toward deeper water, but then he felt movement on the line, a jiggle almost. He turned back, looking down into the pool, and saw the shadow of a good-sized fish looking at his bait. It darted forward and hit it.

He yanked upward hard and whooped when he felt resistance, and his hands were full trying to pull in the fish, keep it tight, and wrap the slack line around the stick, and then he had the flapping fish up out of the water, a black-and-white striped one with whiskers beside its mouth. He clutched it and ran splashing to the beach, afraid it was going to get away.

From down the reef, he heard "All right, Nick!" from Sam.

At the beach he struggled to get the hook out of the fish's mouth. He realized that he'd never fished before, or even touched one of these cool, slippery creatures alive. He almost wished he could take Bea and Sam to Chicago and show them how he knew how to survive on the streets there, because he felt so clumsy and useless here.

Finally, he used a stick to push the hook's point back through the fish's cheek and extracted it without stabbing himself.

The fish was fully dead by then, the sheen gone from its scales.

Sam returned, and Nick felt embarrassed by his excitement over his tiny catch when the younger boy held up a whole row of fish he'd strung on a stick through their gills. "Looks like we'll have enough for a meal."

They'd gotten a driftwood fire started in the fire pit in front of the shack when Bea came back, making him think of a warrior mermaid in her bikini with the spear in her hand, mask on her head, and a metal loop made out of an old coat hanger at her side—flapping with still-live fish.

"Almost lunchtime." She grinned. "I'll show you how to clean fish while Sam does the bird. I bet we'll get all the fish done before he gets that one bird cleaned."

Cleaning the bird wasn't as easy or as pleasant as cleaning fish. Sam gutted the quail, tossing the bloody offal into the ocean as Bea showed Nick how to gut the fish and they worked their way through the pile. He hated plucking birds, and without dipping them in boiling water, the feathers were nearly impossible to pull out. He'd come up with a skinning method for out in the field: he slid the point of the knife just under the skin after he'd cleaned the bird, and pushed it point-first between the meat and the layer of feathers, pushing the knife and pulling on the feathers until he was able to get the bird's skin off.

Bea and Nick had all the rest of the fish cleaned by the time he finished with this laborious, messy process. The bird ended up about the size of a papaya. Oh, well. It would taste good. Sam's mouth watered at the thought of the crispy little drumsticks.

"Granola bars are easier," Bea said, rinsing her hands. "But nothing tastes quite as good as something you've caught, killed, and cooked yourself. Especially when you're really hungry."

"I believe you," Nick said, comically licking his lips. They cooked the fish and grouse on a wire mesh someone had used before, and this time they were able to fill their bellies.

Sam watched Nick eat. The older boy even needed Bea to show him how to get the fish's skin off, how to avoid the tiny bones. He was useless. How was he going to take care of himself when they sailed away on the boat? And Sam could see by the way he looked at Bea that the older boy liked her.

Not as a friend.

It made Sam uncomfortable. He'd always thought Jaden was the one Bea cared about that way, but Bea was sitting a little close to Nick for friends, and surely she didn't have to feed him a piece of fish with her fingers?

They ate most of the fish and saved some for dinner. Sam found an old plastic container and put the fish in it, wrapping it in grasses and burying it under the naupaka tree.

"The flies and bugs won't get to it, and it stays cool that way," he explained to Nick. "So. Bea. You were going to go find the windsurfer sail before we got distracted by getting food. Why don't you do that, and Nick and I can get a little more done on the boat before it gets too hot." Already the sun was directly overhead, beating down on their heads. When it came to the boat, Sam felt confident telling the older kids what to do.

"Sounds good." Bea stood with an abrupt movement and walked down to the water, rinsing her hands.

Sam gestured to Nick. "Come. Let's talk about how to fix up the boat."

The older boy looked after Bea but followed Sam back to the Hobie cat.

"Jaden's her boyfriend, you know," Sam said, clearing a final piece of driftwood away from the boat's hull, feeling a pang of loyal defensiveness toward their longtime friend.

"I get that he wants to be, not that he is," Nick said. Sam looked up into the older boy's level blue eyes. "She can make up her own mind."

Sam frowned. "We're leaving on this boat."

"And I want to come with you."

"I don't think so," Sam said. "You don't have anything we need."

A long silence followed this. Sam knelt in front of the hole in the hull, reached in to pull out some debris that had gotten inside. He felt bad. He'd never said such a mean thing to anyone in his life.

"I hope I can change your mind by the time the boat is ready," Nick said softly, kneeling beside him, digging debris out from under the hull. Sam wouldn't meet his eyes, instead standing up to brush sand off his legs.

"I've made a list of things for the boat. We have a lot of what we need in my dad's workshop, if we can break into it. I think we're going to have to go back to our house."

"And there's where I might be useful," Nick said, with a grin so nice Sam couldn't help smiling back. "How are you going to get the boat from up here down to the water?"

"Didn't think that far ahead."

"Well, here's something I know about. We can put wood down in front of it and pull it over the sand. Like this." Nick lay a stick in the sand and demonstrated.

"Not a bad idea," Sam said. It was going to be interesting to see how Nick could help them break back into their old house. Maybe Nick could be useful after all.

Bea returned from fetching the windsurfer sail, frayed but intact. It was still sleeved onto a carbon-fiber mast and had been used to make a fishing shelter, propped up among tall bushes to cast shade. She'd passed the rig a hundred times, hardly noting it except as another example of how nothing went wasted on Lanai. She'd had to take the sail off the mast, roll it up (difficult with the plastic battens still inside sleeves on the sail), and carry it in front of her on Rainbow as she held one end of the mast and dragged it.

By the time she returned, the afternoon sun was hot. Both boys had taken shelter under a naupaka bush near the boat, and a row of salvaged items decorated the sand in a row in front of the Hobie.

Bea's spirits rose at the sight. Fixing the boat was beginning to look doable, if still daunting. "We're going to do this thing," she whisper/thought to Beosith.

Yes!

The enthusiastic response from the dragon made Bea grin. She could tell he was somewhere cool and dim, waiting for dark. Bea slid off Rainbow, and the mare blew out a breath loudly.

"Okay, girl. Getting some water." She filled the hollowed dent in a nearby stone with water for the horse from one of the jugs they'd brought from the Apucans'. "Did you make a list of what we need?"

"I brought my journal." Sam held it up. "Mainly we need a lot of rope."

She came over, sitting between Sam and Nick and pretending she didn't notice how it felt when her shoulder brushed Nick's. The three of them bent over the journal.

"Nick helped me," Sam said, with a tone of being deliberately fair. There were sketches of a crude rudder and how to attach the mast. Sam's clear brown eyes, so much like their mother's, met Bea's with worry in their depths. "I know where a lot of this stuff is. At our house, in Dad's shed."

The metal shed at the back of their yard held the mower and their father's tools and supplies, many of which would be needed for this project.

"Okay." Bea looked down at the list. "Dad's toolbox is what you need, Sam—and more."

"I know."

"Well, this is all we can do with the boat right now. Let's go set up camp at the fishing shack and take a nap until dark. After we get the stuff from the house, we'll come back."

The three of them settled down to rest through the hot afternoon hours. Nick took off his shirt and lay down on it on the floor of the shack. His back was a painful-looking bright red. Bea took the bottom bunk and Sam the top. It was too hot to cover up with anything, so Bea curled on her side facing the wall and let exhaustion draw her down into heavy slumber.

Bea heard the boys' voices and woke up. She rolled over. Looking outside, she could see the shadows under the naupaka tree stretching long toward the water, and the sun was low over Molokai across the Channel. They'd slept away the hot middle of the day, a rhythm that made sense in the islands.

Bea got up and emptied the two backpacks she and Sam had brought inside the shack, sorting the food items and then digging a hole in the sandy floor and burying them.

"What're you doing?" Nick asked, looking over her shoulder.

"Hiding the food. If someone comes by while we're gone, they'll just think it was their lucky day."

He didn't answer, just began digging a second hole for the rest of the food.

"I think we should wait until after dark to do our raid. I'll keep the pit bull busy while you guys sneak into the shed," Bea said, as Sam joined them. "You'll know better than I what could be useful, and you can each carry one of these backpacks."

"Sure. I know what I need. In and out." Sam's voice rang with false bravado. "Nick helped me with the list, so he knows, too. No problem. I just hope they haven't already broken in and raided it."

"Okay, then. By the time we get to the house, it'll be dark. We can leave Rainbow at the rocks, like last time."

"What are you going to do for a distraction?" Nick asked.

"I'm not sure. I have to check the situation out when we get there." Bea had an idea, but she didn't want to tell them what it was.

"We might as well eat the rest of the fish, or it will go bad," Sam said, and he went to fetch it from its hiding place. Bea walked out onto the beach, wandering up and down until she'd collected a pile of small driftwood chunks. Nick followed.

"Can I help? You planning to throw stuff at the dog?"

"It's an idea. I may use Sam's slingshot."

"Not bad."

He helped her fill a bag with small wood pieces. They fetched Rainbow, and with Sam riding because of his bad foot, the two of them took turns packing with him up the hill to the outcrop of rocks where they tied the mare out.

Sunset was flaming over Maui to the east. They stayed in the shelter of the rocks to wait for full dark. Sitting with her back against one of the warm stones, Nick beside her, Bea's mind went back to Jaden.

Was he wondering where she was? What she was doing? She felt guilty all over again thinking of how they'd left, but she knew his family needed him. The Apucans would never agree with their plan to go to Molokai and might even try to prevent their going.

Nick's firm, bulky shoulder rested against hers. She liked the way he made her feel, almost like there was a magnetic field around him, drawing her into it. But wasn't it Jaden she liked?

Jaden who was always there for her, through all the stuff with their dad. Jaden, her fishing and hunting partner.

Jaden her old friend, who had been looking different to her in the last few months.

It was all so confusing. "Let's get going," she said, standing up abruptly.

"Let's wait until full dark," Nick said, catching her hand and pulling her down beside him. "Just until the sunset's over." He didn't let go of her hand once she was sitting beside him.

The last of the violet-orange sunset streaked the clouds overhead on the other side of Molokai even though the sun was gone. Bea let herself relax, sinking back against the rock, still warm with the afternoon's sun.

She didn't have to figure anything out right now, and for just a little while, she was safe—with Sam leaning on her from one side and Nick on the other and her belly full. She knew there weren't going to be many moments this good in the coming days until they found her aunt and uncle on Molokai, if then.

Finally the sky overhead had gone indigo, the first stars poking holes in the darkness. The moon glimmered on the ever-present ocean and over the uneven ground.

Bea thought she saw a large, rippling shadow not far away, but when she turned her head and tried to focus on it, it seemed to vanish. *Beosith?*

I'm here.

Good. I need you. I have an idea, she thought to the *mo'o* dragon. She sent him a mind picture of what she was thinking, and felt his reluctant agreement. He'd been so absent lately. *Are you doing okay?*

Keeping an eye on you. She saw a tiny flash of light in the darkness, like a firefly, as he winked a lambent eye.

"Seems like it's dark enough now," Nick said. And all Bea's apprehension came flooding back.

They set off across the open, barren field covered in bunchy grass. Bits of black plastic, used for irrigation and ground cover, stuck up from the earth to trip them—mute evidence of the pineapple farming of the island's past. Bea had often wondered why Dole hadn't cleaned it up—but they'd owned the island. They didn't have to. Now some computer billionaire owned Lanai, and with the solar event, what would be happening to all of them?

These and other unhappy thoughts occupied her as they walked toward the grove and slipped under the trees. Bea put her hand forward to touch Sam's shoulder as they moved from the moonlight into the dark of the trees. She let him lead so they wouldn't outpace his limp. Nick was pressed close to her from behind. The leaves inevitably rustled, and a twig broke—not loudly, but enough to make them freeze.

Bea's mind suddenly filled with a moonlit picture of the dog, chained to the corner of the porch, waking. It lifted a big, square head to sniff, and she could see the hair rising on its ruff. In a moment, it would start barking.

Beosith, spying for her. *Thanks, Beosith. I need you for that other thing, too.*

I know. I'm gathering materials. He sent her a sense of how unpleasant they tasted, and she gave a little shudder.

I wouldn't ask if I didn't really need your help.

She crept forward as close as she could get, within sight of the house, and slid her backpack off in the darkness.

"Go on, guys," she whispered. "Sam, give me your slingshot."

"Why?"

"Just do it." Sam handed over the slingshot and bag of weights, and he and Nick melted away from her side, heading toward the back of the grove near the cave where they'd sheltered and the shed.

She'd made her preparations at the beach—chunks of driftwood sprinkled with oil she'd taken from the Apucans filling a ziplock bag. She crept one tree closer to the house and squatted down behind its roots.

The dog still hadn't barked.

Beosith rustled up beside her, a shadow darker than black. She smelled the sulfur and horse dung of fire's raw materials on his breath. His eyes, muted in stealth mode, shone only enough for her to see he was right beside her.

Are you sure you want to try this?

Yes, but I'm not sure how we're going to do it. She took out a chunk of oily wood, holding it by the dry end. In the dark it was hard to see, and suddenly the oily wood seemed to burst into flame, singeing her fingers—and she hadn't seen the dragon do anything yet. She dropped the chunk of wood, fumbling for the slingshot as flame flared up among the leaves.

The dog burst into its bellowing barking.

Bea grabbed the end of the wood that wasn't on fire and set it in the leather thong, but she couldn't get leverage to shoot with the brand already lit. The chunk fizzled weakly into the yard and rolled in front of the pit bull. The dog stopped barking to look at it.

New strategy. She set the next one, unlit, into the thong and pulled it back. "Light it now, Beosith," she whispered.

This time she saw a ball of blue heat shoot from the dragon's nostrils. It flew by her crude missile, landing in the leaves, but it did catch the wood on fire. Bea shot the flaming bit of wood as high and as far as she could.

It landed on the ancient cedar shake roof, rolling down to land in the gutter, sputtering out. The flaming chunk on the ground in front of the dog went out, and the animal resumed barking even as she stomped on the leaves catching fire at her feet. She heard thumping in the house as the Boyz woke up.

The third flaming brand settled onto the flat roof over the porch, burning merrily. The fourth and fifth also stuck and kept going.

"Go, guys, hurry," she muttered.

I think we have enough distraction going, Beosith said.

That's when Bea realized the fire was getting out of control.

18

NICK KEPT A HAND ON Sam's shoulder, following the boy through the trees. Even in the darkness he could tell that Sam knew the way. They heard the dog begin barking, so Bea had begun her distraction. By then they were at the edge of the yard closest to the locked toolshed. There was no more cover.

"Go," Nick said, giving the younger boy a push. He'd lifted Sam's Leatherman out of the younger boy's pocket without him noticing, and the metal blade gleaming dully in the moonlight felt reassuring to Nick. As long as the Boyz didn't use guns, he'd have a good chance against them— he'd learned how to use a knife from Dodger.

While Sam fumbled with the combination lock, which was still on the shed door, Nick faced the back of the house—and jerked in surprise as he saw a flaming ball of wood hit the top of the roof and come bouncing down in their direction. Bea had chosen an undeniably effective distraction. His heart thudded with fear for her.

"Hurry," he whispered.

Sam got the lock undone and rushed into the darkness of the shed. Nick saw the younger boy pause and grab something—and then it flared into light. A barbeque lighter, not mechanical enough to have been fried in the solar event. In its flickering light, Sam held up the list they'd made. "Help me find these things!"

Glue

Resin

Nails/screws

Wire (plastic coated)

Duct tape

Varnish/paint

Rope/string

Rubber tubing

Hammer

Screwdriver

Wire cutters

Pliers

Clamps

Nick stayed as close as he could to the door while frantically feeling along the shelves and workbench for potentially useful items. Sam kept the barbeque lighter and went for his dad's toolbox, a big wooden contraption with a sticky lid that Nick finally had to hit to get open. They scooped tools into the backpacks, along with a bag of nails, a bottle of industrial glue, a metal canister that Sam whispered was the varnish. Nick found a huge coil of rope on the lowest shelf and stuffed it into his own backpack, filling it completely.

"That's it. We have to go," he whispered, spooked by the red glow flickering into the shed. "We've got to get Bea out of there."

They ran out of the shed and into the trees with no attempt to hide the noise. Nick slid the knife out of his pocket and held it ready. They hurried to Bea and were able to see easily by the burning light of the roof.

The Boyz had run into the yard, waving their guns and holding their baggy pants up, swearing and yelling in consternation. Someone brought out a bucket of water and tried to throw it up onto the roof even as another corner caught fire with a little whoosh and an explosion of sparks.

Another bucket of water tried, and failed, to reach the burning area. The fire was out of control. Bea stood just behind the trunk of the tree, the fire flickering on her face, the slingshot dangling from her hand. Nick tugged on her elbow as she watched the Boyz frantically hauling their possessions out into the yard, apparently giving up on suppressing the blaze.

"You set the house on fire, Bea." Sam's eyes were wide in the light of the leaping flames beside her.

"It was an accident." She turned to them and her eyes were so wide there was a white ring around them. Her lips seemed to be stiff as she said, "I thought they'd put it out. I thought it would just keep them busy."

"We have to go." Nick tugged on her arm again, but she was unresponsive. He grabbed her stiff body and turned her away from the blaze, half carrying, half dragging her into the darkness under the trees. She seemed paralyzed, her legs dragging.

"Bea! We have to go!" Sam, ahead of them, sounded frantic.

Finally Bea's legs started working and Nick was able to pull her through darkness lit by a wavering reddish glow from the burning house.

Sam peered off the top bunk to check on Bea as he lay down in the fishing shack. She lay motionless on the bottom bunk. Her eyes were open. Wide and blank, spooky. The light of the moon outside reflected off the whites, and she didn't blink. Nick was a dark shadow on the ground beside her.

Sam rolled onto his back, stared at the splintery wooden ceiling just a foot or two over his head. He closed eyes gritty with smoke and tiredness.

Bea had been like a robot getting back to the fishing shack. Nick had had to lead her back to Rainbow, pulling to get her to run, even carrying her part of the way. Sam had been terrified they'd let the dog off the chain and it would come after them, or that the Boyz, ousted from their hideout, would be looking for revenge.

He'd untied Rainbow and mounted. Nick got Bea up on the horse in front of Sam by lifting her up. They rode away as fast as they could in the dark. Sam kept Bea on by physically holding her in front of him. It was a hard ride back to the fishing shack holding Bea while still wearing the heavy backpack laden with stuff from the shed, but he didn't envy Nick trotting alongside them, stumbling in the dark and burdened by his heavy backpack. Away from the immediate threat of the Boyz and the dog, Sam had shouted at Bea, trying to snap her out of it. He'd even slapped her cheeks until Nick made him stop.

"She's in shock," Nick said. "She didn't mean for the fire to get so bad."

Bea must be feeling terrible about burning the house down.

Sam hadn't had much at the house that he cared about except for his comic collection. But Bea had more stuff, sentimental things like their mom's nightgown and the photo album with all their pictures. He knew she kept the nightgown under her pillow and the photos under her bed.

At least they hadn't owned the house. It was a rental, like most of the homes on the island. He could only hope Bea was better in the morning.

It seemed like the next minute he woke up, and sunshine was a bright lance coming in the door. He shot up, hit his head on the ceiling, fell back, and rolled over to look at Bea.

She was asleep. She wasn't lying the way she usually did, though. Her arms were at her sides, soldier-straight, and she'd made no move to get into her sleeping bag. She looked frozen—but at least her eyes were shut.

Nick was gone.

Sam slid off the bunk, tiptoed over to the food cache, dug in, and grabbed a granola bar. He picked up the full backpack of supplies he'd taken from the shed. Might as well get started on the boat before it got too hot.

The sand was chilly with early day as he walked back to the Hobie and the assembled pile of potentially useful items. Nick's full backpack from the night before had been placed beside the pile they'd made.

Sam turned to look around with a hand sheltering his eyes. He could see Nick out on the reef with the fishing line in his hand. The older boy raised a hand and Sam waved back.

Nick had earned his place with them, just as he'd said he would. He couldn't help liking the Mainland boy for his courage and help. Even if Nick didn't know much about surviving here, he seemed to be learning fast. Getting fish was a good idea and Sam's stomach rumbled in agreement with it.

Sam turned back to the boat project. He decided to start with the rudder, since it required the most assembly and he was going to need Nick to help with bigger things, like the mast. Unlike Bea, he'd had a few sailing lessons with his uncle Buzz on Molokai. Uncle's fishing boat was outboard driven, but sometimes he used a drift sail to save fuel when he was trolling, and Sam had learned a few of the basics from helping rig and steer the boat.

Hobie cats usually had dual rudders on a hinged pole attaching them, but Sam thought he could rig a single rudder that would work. He took the largest square of plywood and nailed it to a pole. He stood it up at the back of the aluminum frame, where their trampoline platform, if they could rig one, would be located.

There seemed to be little way to connect his crude rudder with the smooth aluminum of the frame. He needed something he could nail.

He found a two-by-four among the detritus and, using rope, lashed it onto the metal frame.

He opened his backpack and took out the items he'd been able to retrieve from his dad's shed. He attached hinges to the pole with the rudder nailed to it, and he was screwing the last screw in to attach the pole to the two-by-four on the frame when he heard, "So this is what you've been doing."

He whirled, the screwdriver held defensively, to see the grinning face of his friend Jeremy.

The boy's face was pink with exertion—he'd probably gotten out of bed before dawn to get down here by the time the sun came up, and his black hair, always a little unruly, pointed in various directions. Jeremy had never looked better to Sam, and he almost hugged his friend.

"Hey. We're fixing up this boat."

"I see that. Can I help?"

"Sure. Hold this pole; stabilize it." He was able to press down hard with the screwdriver and finish attaching the hinges must faster with Jeremy holding the pole steady. "Where's Jaden?" Wherever Jeremy was, Jaden was sure to be there, too.

"It was Jaden's idea to come check on you guys. He's back at the shack, trying to wake Bea up. What's wrong with her?"

"We had to sneak back to our house to get the stuff for the boat. Bea lit the house on fire by accident and burned it down. I dunno—I guess she's in shock. She was acting all weird last night, getting back here." Sam straightened up and pushed sweaty hair out of his eyes. "I hope he can snap her out of it."

Bea felt something soft on her mouth. It was gentle, and pleasant, and she didn't mind—in fact, it was very nice—but she felt the gray receding.

That scared her. The gray was there to keep her safe, to keep her from knowing something terrible. In a sudden panic, she lashed out and sat up, banging her head on the splintery underside of the bunk bed.

Jaden was sitting on the floor next to her, a hand pressed to his cheek, eyes watering as he rubbed his face.

"What are you doing here?" she cried, swinging her legs off the bunk.

"I was trying to wake you up." He looked down. He was red to the tips of his ears. It appeared she must have hit him. "Glad you're awake."

"You tried to kiss me."

"I'm sorry. I shouldn't have. But nothing was working to wake you up." His face flamed even redder than where she'd slapped him.

"I wish you'd left me alone." Tears rose, hot and stinging, behind her eyes as she stood up and walked out of the fishing shack. "I burned our house down."

"Oh, crap—I mean, wow," Jaden said, getting up to follow her out into the cool sand under the naupaka tree. She sat down, looking out across the smooth, sparkling early-morning water on the reef, lacy around the edges with foam. The Kalohi Channel was as smooth as glass, and Molokai, all orangey-violet curves and shadows, looked close enough to touch. Nick was just bringing up a fat fish from the pool she'd showed him yesterday, and he whooped with triumph.

They waved to him as he splashed in to shore.

"What happened?" Jaden asked.

"We needed stuff for rebuilding the boat." Bea told him about the salvage expedition. "I don't know what I was thinking."

"I bet you wanted them out of there," Jaden said, his jaw set and eyes narrowed. "I bet you wanted the Boyz gone so bad you were willing to burn the house down rather than let them have it."

Nick had reached the shore and was now struggling to get the hook out of the mouth of a good-sized papio, a silver jack that would cook up nice over their fire.

"It was an accident. I was just thinking of distracting them. I thought they'd be able to put the fire out." She considered. "But you might be onto something there."

Bea turned, feeling the cold grains of sand against her legs, the cool of early morning touching her skin as she looked at her friend. She liked the way the sun struck Jaden's deep brown eyes, lighting his long lashes with their almost-blond tips. She wished she'd enjoyed his kiss instead of freaking out. She could have pretended not to know what he was doing, just gently woken up, or pretended to keep sleeping, and he might have done it again.

She touched her lips, then dropped her hand. Her stomach growled loudly. He grinned, that bright flash that always made her smile, too. "Hungry?"

"Always, these days."

Nick came up with his fish. "Breakfast," he said proudly.

"It's a start," Jaden said. "See you're learning a few skills."

"Helps to have the right equipment," Nick quoted with a grin. "Glad to see you feeling better, Bea."

"Yeah." Bea ducked her head in embarrassment. She could hardly remember getting back to the shack, or anything but realizing the house was burning. "I'll get some firewood."

"I brought some food from the house. We thought you guys might be hungry," Jaden said, unzipping his backpack.

"We're doing okay that way," Bea said, laying the fire in the pit as Nick cleaned his fish with the Leatherman knife. She wondered how he'd gotten it. He must have borrowed it from Sam. "We went fishing yesterday, but we're going to have to do that every day or eat the stuff we want to take on the boat."

"What boat?"

Bea told Jaden as he opened his backpack to take out a couple of homemade fish musubi: compacted cooked rice, topped by a fish filet, all of it wrapped in nori. The chewy, salty, fishy mix of flavors was delicious as she munched down the Japanese variation on a sandwich. Jaden handed one to Nick, too.

"Damn, this is good," Nick mumbled around a mouthful. "Never expected it to be so tasty."

Bea set Nick's catch on the wire rack over the fire. "Let's cook this and then get over to the boat, and you can see what I'm talking about. I bet Sam's already working hard."

They joined the younger boys, carrying the cooked fish on a pile of leaves. Bea looked over Sam's adaptation of a rudder: a square of plywood nailed to a pole, hinged on to a spar tied on to the aluminum frame. Sam looked up at their arrival, face flushed with excitement, and something she didn't remember seeing before—confidence.

"Check it out, Bea," he said, demonstrating that by turning the pole attached to the "rudder" back and forth, the square of wood scythed through the sand. "I think this will work."

"Good job, bro," Bea said, feeling bad about her behavior last night.

"Glad you brought food!"

Typical little brother. She smiled with relief. "We've got a great breakfast with what Nick caught and Jaden brought from home."

They took a break, sitting in the shade. Everyone ate while Sam excitedly shared his plans for the boat—mast and sail from the windsurfer, inserted through the mast mount hole in the aluminum frame and held in place with rope. Trampoline platform resurrected from washed-up nets. Rudder already under construction.

"Seems like you've done a lot, but there's still more to do," Jaden said. He sat in the sand with them, resting his wiry brown arms on his knees as he looked at the boat. "The question I have is—why are you doing this? You guys can stay with us as long as you want."

Sam took a big bite of his musubi, his eyes down, leaving Bea to answer.

"I know, Jaden. Your family is awesome. But—we need to get over there to our aunty and uncle's house, be with our own family. Maybe that's where Dad went, too."

Jaden tightened his mouth. "Your dad left you guys. You should stay with us. We'll look out for you."

Sam and Jeremy stood up and walked away, fiddling with the rudder—apparently the conversation was too much for them. Nick went down to the ocean and washed his hands. Bea took another bite of her musubi and chewed, swallowing past the lump in her throat.

"It's not you guys—it's about family." Bea might be mad at her dad—and if she took the time to think about it, she knew she was—but she couldn't find the words to explain. "We really just want to get to our aunty and uncle's house. We belong there. We don't want to be a burden to you."

"Sorry. I understand. If it were me, I'd want to be with my family, too." Jaden's eyes were downcast. "I'll just miss you; that's all."

"I know. I'll miss you, too." All the words Bea couldn't figure out how to say lay silently between them, and she fiddled with the ti leaf the rice snack had been wrapped in.

"Is Nick going with you?"

"I don't know."

"Well, you should find out."

Jeremy and Sam had begun hauling the sail and mast over to the boat.

"Time to get back to work," Bea said, standing up. "Maybe we can even sail out of here tomorrow."

19

SAM AWOKE LONG BEFORE IT was morning. They had planned to get everything set and move the boat across the shallow expanse of reef and take off at first light, before the wind really kicked up across the Kalohi Channel.

He rolled over and looked below.

"What?" Bea was awake. "Can we go yet?"

"I think so." Even without his little battery-operated watch, burned out like everything else in the solar event, Sam could sense a change in the light that told him dawn was coming.

He slid out of the bunk and she out of hers. Nick woke silently and stood, shaking out his clothes as they rolled their nylon sleeping bags up for the last time. Sam used the barbeque lighter for a couple of seconds, preserving the fuel, to shine a light around and make sure he'd packed everything in the shack.

They trudged through the cool sand to the Hobie. With the five of them pushing, yesterday they'd been able to roll it across driftwood logs as Nick had suggested and position it just in front of the tiny purling waves that rolled across the shallow expanse of the early-morning reef.

The boat looked a little *kapakahi*, a Hawaiian word for mishmash or "anykine." But to Sam, the resurrected Hobie was evidence he could do something. Bad foot or not, youngest or not, he'd been the one to direct the others yesterday.

The mast rose straight and proud, lashed in several places to the platform with the super strong climbing rope Bea had found in the plane luggage. The windsurfer sail, while a lot smaller than a sixteen-foot catamaran would normally need, should still be more than adequate to get them across the nine open ocean miles to Molokai in just a few hours. He'd rigged it with rope going from the eye of the boom to clamps on either corner of the trampoline frame. They'd restrung the seven-foot square of the trampoline with pieces of fishing net woven with the rope Nick had lugged from Dad's shed to make a slightly sagging but sturdy sitting area.

All five of them had tried climbing aboard and jumping up and down, and the platform had held. That had been the last moment that they'd laughed together, just before Jeremy and Jaden had said goodbye, taking Rainbow with them. Sam tried not to think about how hard that had been. Bea had cried in the dark in her sleeping bag. He and Nick had pretended not to hear.

As they'd planned, they loaded four gallon jugs of water on board, way more than they'd need for the brief sail across the Channel. Sam had made that crossing in just a couple of hours in his uncle's fishing boat, but Jaden said it might take up to four hours with their small sail—he'd sailed it before on an outrigger canoe. Still, it was always better to be safe than sorry when dealing with the ocean.

Sam strung the gallon jugs on a loop of rope and tied them down while Bea stowed their sleeping bags, backpacks, and food supplies in the netting near the mast. She wrapped the items in a large piece of tarpaulin and tied it down, hopefully enough to keep any overspray out. Nick pulled the last of the wood out from under the gunnels.

Lastly, they stowed their fishing gear aft near the rudder along with an old oar and paddle. Bea planned to troll for fish all the way to Molokai so they'd arrive with plenty to eat.

Sam hopped down and walked around, looking for anything else they might need or have missed. He spotted the single life preserver Bea had brought from one of the other fishing shacks. It was one of the Styrofoam ring types used on boats, printed with LUCKY LADY on the sun-shot canvas cover.

It was better than nothing if one of them fell overboard, and hopefully they wouldn't need it. He found an extra hank of rope, tied on the ring and attached it to the mast, stowing it on board.

Bea hopped down from the boat. "I'm glad I said goodbye to Rainbow last night. I think it would be really hard to do that this morning."

"I know," Sam said. The sweet-faced chestnut mare had looked puzzled when Jaden and Jeremy mounted her instead of Bea and Sam. She refused to move until Bea yelled and smacked her on the rump, making the mare jump into a trot that carried the other two boys out of sight. "They'll take good care of her."

"I know. I just…" She sighed. "I love that horse."

"We'll see her again. Let's get going."

"I guess this is the moment of truth." Nick stood on the beach beside them. "Can I come with you?"

Bea's fern-green eyes were wide, innocent. "I think we can use his strength," she said to Sam, pretend casual. Sam looked at Nick. The older boy's face was carefully blank, but Sam could see how much he wanted to come in the way he leaned forward.

"You said you'd earn your place with us, and you did," Sam said.

"Yes!" Nick exclaimed, and they all laughed in relief. Sam realized in that moment that if Nick had chosen to, they couldn't have stopped him from coming anyway. He was bigger than both of them combined.

The deep blue of night was giving way to violet-gray, lightening dramatically over Maui off to the east. The first yellow glow topped the West Maui mountain range and reached across to warm the dark of Molokai, their destination, into a shape like a humpback whale rising from the depths of the ocean. The nine miles of water between Lanai and Molokai glittered smooth as obsidian. Surely it was just a short distance. They'd be seeing their cousins in no time.

The three of them got behind the frame of the boat and pushed it down into the water. Several of the long branches of driftwood they'd used to roll the boat to the edge remained and they rolled beneath the twin hulls until the boat rested on the reef.

The reef stretched before them, fifty yards of flat water just inches deep, moguled with tide pools, coral heads, and lacy at the far edge where it met the sea with a necklace of foamy breaking waves.

They were halfway across the reef, applying muscle to the back of the frame as the hulls caught in a pool again, when Sam heard a voice call, "Wait!"

They stopped and turned to see who was coming.

Bea's heart thumped hard, leaping up into her throat—not just from the exertion, but from the sight of Jaden running toward them down the beach.

Good, Beosith said, from somewhere watery and deep nearby. *The boy will be a help.*

Jaden already wore his tabis and carried a heavy-looking backpack, but he hardly slowed, splashing at a trot across the reef until he reached them.

"I'm coming with you." He slung the backpack into the net of the trampoline.

"What?" Sam said. "Your parents will never let you."

"I left them a note. It's going to be fine. Figured you could use an extra pair of hands that know the ocean."

"I don't know why you think this is a good idea. Your parents are going to freak," Bea said. Nick was silent.

"They won't. In fact, I heard Papa talking last night about wanting to find out what's going on in the rest of the world. I figure I'll go over with you, help you get settled, see what's going on, catch a boat back, give everyone a report." He brushed sweaty hair off his forehead, brown eyes sparkling with excitement. "Didn't really think you could leave me behind, did you?" he whispered to Bea.

"Guess not." She turned away, smiling. "Hope you brought your own food."

"Sure did, and some extra for you guys, too. And water." He unzipped the loaded backpack to show them. "You don't know how tempting it was to ride Rainbow down here this morning, but I couldn't put Jeremy in the position of taking her back and having to cover for me."

"So you admit you're going to be in trouble for this," Bea said, as the four of them put their shoulders to the aluminum frame, lifting the hull out of the pool it had been stuck in.

"Oh yeah. But I'm hoping the news I come back with is so good, they'll forgive me."

The light craft, no more than three hundred and fifty pounds spread over sixteen feet of double hull, was easy to push after they dislodged it. At the edge of the reef, before the imposing deep blue of the Kalohi Channel began, Sam clambered aboard and loosened the windsurfer sail. It belled to port, catching the slight early-morning breeze, and the craft lifted forward.

"Get on!" Sam yelled, and the three teens each scrambled onto the hulls and into the trampoline. Sam took a seat on the trampoline, taking hold of his makeshift tiller in one hand and the rope running through a cleat that controlled the sail in the other.

"We go!" Jaden's grin was wide as the moon and twice as shiny. Bea couldn't help laughing with excitement, and Nick grinned, trailing a hand in the smooth water as he leaned out from the hull.

Bea crawled forward and stowed Jaden's backpack inside the cocoon of tarpaulin covering their other gear. She looked through the four-inch holes in the netting to the dark blue of the ocean below, sliding swiftly by—and deep beneath, a long black shadow tracked them.

Her heart seized, her hands stilled—and she heard Beosith's voice in her mind. *It's me—I didn't leave you.*

"Oh, thank God," she whispered, watching the shadow of the dragon arrow along beneath them, unbelievably graceful and swift as a porpoise. The breeze freshened against her cheeks, and the smell of salt water filled her with profound happiness.

"What do you see down there?" Jaden asked. He was rigging three short, sturdy fishing poles for trolling, tying large hooks into steel leaders and baiting them with opihi flesh.

"Thought I saw a dolphin. Must have just been a shadow," Bea said.

"We'll probably see dolphins," Sam said. "We usually did when Uncle and I went out in the Channel."

Bea looked back at Lanai. Nick was looking at it, too, and they smiled at each other. The island towered behind them, a smoothly rounded dome brightening to ochre at the crest with the sunrise. Rain-carved gullies were deep purple shadows in the dim light, the crest of the island with its crown of cloud unexpectedly beautiful and as dear as family to Bea.

She raised her hand in a silent goodbye.

20

NICK TOOK THE FISHING RIG Jaden handed him. It was nothing more than a stout stick with a ball of line wrapped around it and a big baited hook with a couple of weights above it..

"Drop it down and just let the momentum of the boat pull out the line," Bea said, turning around in the net and letting hers pay out behind the cat.

Nick pretended to be fumbling a bit just so he could look around some more. He'd never been sailing before, never been on the ocean. He'd been on the pier, looked at Lake Michigan, which was big enough to pretend it was the ocean, but it didn't smell like this. Didn't have this vitality, vibrancy of color, sense of life. Even as he looked toward their destination, he saw a plume of water go high into the air.

"What's that?" He pointed.

"Whale," Bea said casually.

Nick couldn't imagine being casual about something like that. He wondered how close they'd get to the whale, if he'd be able to see it, if it was dangerous. He bit his tongue on his questions, catching Jaden's contemptuous glance.

"Fish on!" Jaden yelled suddenly, setting his hook just as something hit Bea's line as well. She yelped, yanking the tip of her stick up to keep the line tight.

Both of them were fully occupied with fish when the little craft hit the first wind line, and the cat heeled hard to one side, surging forward and beginning to lift onto one hull.

"Get to starboard!" Sam yelled. "I need your weight on this side!"

Bea gave a cry as she lost her grip on the fishing pole and her balance, and Nick thought he was going to have to pitch the rescue ring in after her but she caught herself and clung to the ropes, emitting a string of bad words as her makeshift fishing rig vanished in their wake.

"Don't swear!" Jaden teased in a high-pitched imitation of Bea's voice.

"Starboard!" Sam yelled again. Nick wasn't sure what that meant, but he imitated Bea and Jaden as they crawled over to the far right side of the craft, their weight counterbalancing the pressure on the sail and pushing the hull back into the water.

Jaden was still fighting his fish, and he brought it in close to the boat. Nick reached for the other boy's line to steady it. He could see it was a blunt-faced, long, tapered shape.

"Mahimahi," Jaden said, grinning. "Good catch so close to shore. That's how deep the Channel is. Mahi like the open ocean."

Jaden worked it in close to the hull, chortling with excitement, and Bea wrapped her hand in a piece of tarpaulin and reached over, grabbing the steel leader and pulling the fish up as Nick grabbed the thrashing tail with his bare hands.

Jaden and Nick lifted as Bea heaved. Together they tossed the three-foot fish, flickering rainbows of distressed bioluminescence, into the net of the trampoline.

Nick gazed at the fish, wonder thickening his tongue. He'd never seen anything like the lively flashes of color zinging back and forth along its greenish length, and it filled him with something like awe—a feeling he hid as Jaden dispatched the fish with a quick blow to the head with the haft of his knife. The mahimahi went limp and silver, rainbows chasing across its body a few more times as the life ebbed from it.

Sam held the tiller steady as Bea took Nick's unused hand line and tossed it behind the boat. "Mahi are school fish," she explained. "We should keep our lines out while they're hitting."

A few minutes later Bea brought their second fish to the rail, a bullet-shaped, razor-finned, pewter-colored aku. It was only five pounds or so, and she was able to flip it into the netting.

"We can make some mean sashimi." She dispatched the aku and put it with the mahi.

Nick was the only one watching the fish go from silver to gray as Bea and her friend tossed their lines back out. He tried not to mind that he'd missed his chance to get his line in the water.

The Hobie cat felt good to Sam, responsive to his hand on the makeshift tiller, the sail filled but the wind pressure stayed solid, moving them forward at about the speed of a man jogging. He wondered how many "knots" that was and why sailing was measured in knots anyway.

If only it would keep up like this—but Sam knew they were still in the island's wind shadow, and just a couple of hundred yards ahead he could see a sharp demarcation between the smooth water they traversed now and the ruffled wind tunnel ahead that never really turned off, even in the cool of night.

Sam prepared by trimming the sail in tighter, tying it down to the frame near him. Both Bea and Jaden tossed trolling lines out on either side of him while Nick clung to the ropes. Sam looked ahead at Molokai, and the early-morning light brought it suddenly into high relief, a greener, softer, wider flank than the barren red earth of Lanai. So close…Surely they'd be there in just an hour or two.

The wind hit with a smack like a giant cat's paw, and Sam was very glad he'd tied the sail down because he needed his full strength to cling to the tiller. He tried to hold it steady as the wind and current pushed unrelentingly to port. He was glad he'd had the older kids sit on the starboard side as the cat trembled and tried to lift. The wood vibrated beneath his hands, shuddering, and for the first time he wondered if it was sturdy enough. He thought of his nails, four of them holding the square of plywood to the tiller pole… Maybe he should have added five.

He was the only one to feel the sharp crack and the sudden loose sensation that told him the rudder was gone.

Bea lurched a little as a gust seemed to catch the sail, but she had her knees dug into the netting holes as she threw out her hand line, in a hurry to get another mahi. She held the stick loosely in both hands, letting the line spool out behind the boat—which, now that she noticed, seemed to be curving rather hard to port, running almost directly downwind.

"I lost the rudder." Sam's sun-pinkened face had gone pale as he wiggled the pole, demonstrating the lack of responsiveness. "I think we're going to have some trouble aiming for the other shore."

Bea swiveled to look at the bulk of Molokai. Dead ahead was a forbiddingly rugged expanse of rocky cliffs, now almost parallel to them.

"This is not good." Jaden wound up his line and stowed it. "We could blow right past the island."

"What can we do?" Bea felt a chill break out over her body. She didn't know anything about sailing—her beloved "old school" uncle Buzz, who'd taught Sam all he knew, hadn't taken her out on the ocean at all. Her total boating experience was limited to a whale watch with her school class and ferry rides. Actual time spent on a sailing craft was a big fat zero.

"We can let the sail out. It's sleeved onto the mast. We can't take it off or let it down—but if we just let it out totally and tie it down, we'll slow down," Sam said.

Bea rolled up her hand line, thinking. "Sam, we have that paddle you put on board. Why don't you try steering with that?" She tucked her hand line away and pulled back the tarp to show the old oar they'd picked up on the beach, along with a splintery canoe paddle, stowed among the backpacks.

"Good idea." Sam untied the sail. It flapped dangerously back and forth as he took the oar and plunged it into the water.

Bea looked worriedly at the water below. The Hobie might be moving slightly slower, but not much, and she didn't like the way the shoreline seemed to be whizzing by without them getting any closer. She spotted Beosith again, still tracking them, a long, slim, fast-moving dark shape in the water.

We might be in trouble.

I know. I'll help if I need to.

I'll let you know when.

Sam handed Bea the rope attached to the sail cleat. "Can you wrap that around the mast so it doesn't flap so much? Just the wind running is pushing us along, and if we can just keep going at an angle, we should still be okay."

Nick, trying to help, took the other paddle and held it in the water beside Sam. "Like this?"

"Yeah. If we both do it, it should work better."

Bea lashed the sail awkwardly around the mast as Sam dug out the oar and stuck it in the water as deep as he could, directing Nick to do the same. Without any way to attach it, Sam ended up having to sit facing backward with the oar between his knees as he tried to get some turn for the craft.

Their efforts didn't seem to be changing the craft's trajectory much, but at least the boat's parallel trajectory had slowed down. Bea saw Sam's thin, wiry arms trembling with effort as he held the oar as deep in the water as he could. Bea wondered how long the boys could keep it up.

She decided she might as well gut the fish. She put her hand out to Jaden.

"Your knife."

He handed it to her with one hand, tightening the rope holding the sail to the mast. "Do you think it's working?"

Bea shook her head. "Not yet."

She turned toward the bow of the boat, held down the aku and hacked off its head, tossing it overboard followed by a handful of guts. She did the same to the mahi, and then leaned off the boat to trail her hands in the water, rinsing them off as she watched the water and considered. "It seems like we're going slower, and we're kind of heading toward land now. But I can see the end of the island—it looks like we might still shoot past it."

"We can't." Jaden's voice was tight. "There's nothing past Molokai for a thousand miles until Tahiti."

Bea looked back down for the reassuring shape of her `aumakua far below—and this time, she saw several small, sleek black forms circling and zigzagging back and forth.

Sharks.

And she'd brought them, by throwing fish guts over the side. She'd drawn them right to her `aumakua.

21

SAM WAS TURNED BACK TOWARD Lanai, the wind in his face and both hands on the oar, legs wrapped around to stabilize it. He found himself praying. *Please, God. Please help us get to land.* He turned his head to see Bea washing her hands in the water off the side of the craft.

"No!" she cried suddenly.

"What?" Jaden, kneeling across from her, peered down into the water. "What're you looking at?"

"Sharks," Bea said. "My fault. Dummy. Why'd I throw the guts in the water?"

Sam saw Nick recoil, his big hands clutching the paddle. "Sharks?" He craned his neck, looking into the water.

"Oh, shoots." Now Sam spotted the sharks, too, and they were moving a lot faster than usual, whipping through the water below them.

Their craft was moving slow enough for the sleek fish to keep up easily. He spotted black tips and white tips, around six feet long, circling and zigzagging—but more concerning, at least three tiger sharks twice the others' size cruised by, their barred backs blending with the water. They swam almost lazily, their tails hardly moving, and still effortlessly kept up.

The sharks' frenzy seemed to have drawn something bigger—a dark shape at least as large as a pony, but with a long tail and neck, deep in the water below them. There were rumors that great white sharks sometimes came into Hawaiian waters—but this shark's shape was all wrong.

Sam's knuckles went white on the oar. He'd always had a special fear of sharks since a baby hammerhead washed up on the beach and supposedly dead hadn't been. His browned thumb bore the half-moon scar of his curiosity.

"It doesn't matter. We're safe up here." Sam fought his instinct to pull the oar out of the water—as if the sharks could somehow reach him through it.

The water below erupted in a flurry of splashing motion—and Bea screamed, "No!" again, pulling out the three-prong spear from the cache under the tarp and leaning out to stab at the milling sharks.

She must have hit one, too, because the spear was almost yanked out of her hands. This time she cocked it, twisting the rubber cord around her wrist and taking careful aim.

"Leave them alone!" Jaden shouted to her. Sam smelled fear on him. "You're only making it worse!"

The melee went on, and Sam found himself pressed close to Nick, a worried frown on the older boy's face as he watched Bea. It appeared this might be true, because the two sharks she'd hit were bleeding, and now their brethren turned on them to attack, leaving the largest one pulling away and swimming out in front.

The windborne drift of the Hobie moved them past the spot where the sharks continued to frenzy.

Bea took one last shot and hit another one—but this time, the rubber cord caught on her hand, and the shark on the end of her spear yanked her into the water.

She was there one second, leaning over the side of the boat, then gone beneath the waves with hardly a splash. She didn't even scream.

"No!" Nick yelled. Bea bobbed up behind the boat, and Sam saw something he'd never seen before—his sister's eyes round with terror. She struck out, swimming after them and causing a disturbing amount of splash.

"Throw her the ring!" Sam yelled, pointing at the Lucky Lady life preserver near the mast. Jaden grabbed it and threw it with a huge heave. The ring spiraled through the air and splashed down at least six feet from Bea. She swam harder, but the momentum of the Hobie tugged the ring along, bobbing just out of reach.

Even with the sail down, the craft was moving faster than Bea could swim. Behind her seal-dark head, Sam saw fins leaving the fray and heading in her direction.

"Swim, Bea! Swim hard!" Sam screamed, but even as his sister swam faster and harder than he'd ever seen, Sam knew it wasn't going to be enough.

Jaden flipped open his jackknife and moved aft, preparing to dive in as Sam and Nick paddled backward with the oar, trying to slow the Hobie.

Bea felt an almost superhuman effort take over as adrenaline pumped through her system and she swam after the boat.

Speed was the only thing that could save her now. The ring was just ahead, a blur of orange. A blur that still wouldn't save her, she thought, even as she felt something hit her leg. It was just an experimental bump, but she knew the rasp of the shark's sandpapery hide had frayed off her bare skin.

Everything slowed down. The world narrowed to nothing but the orange ring she was striving for. Clear, warm water was all around her, stinging her eyes—and she was in utter danger. The water around her suddenly boiled with activity, and Bea shut her eyes, still swimming but not wanting to see what came next.

It would be bad enough to feel it.

But this time the force that hit her was from below, and it lifted her straight up above the surface of the water, propelling her forward.

Grab on.

Beosith! She wrapped herself around the water dragon's slippery body, and his tail lashed, tossing their pursuers away. His legs churned like a powerboat, heaving her forward until she grabbed the orange ring. She could feel the motion all around her in the water as Beosith drove off the sharks.

Jaden and Nick, red-faced with effort, hauled her into the boat. Nick grabbed her under the arms and heaved her aboard, falling backward as he did so that she landed right on top of him.

Bea shut her eyes, gasping with exhaustion and relief to be safe. She felt Nick's arms still tight around her, their slippery, wet bodies clasped together, and she was in no hurry to change the situation. Being hugged had never felt so good.

"Bea, your leg is bleeding!" Jaden's voice was thick with alarm. Bea turned her head to look down at her calf, aware of a burning sensation. The skin was abraded and blood oozed from a fist-sized area. Nick had sat up with her, and he frowned. "Any other injuries?"

Jaden ripped off his none-too-clean T-shirt and put it over her leg.

"No. Thanks. I'm fine." She checked her extremities to be sure, and relief made her voice squeaky. *Thank you, Beosith. I owe you my life.*

That's what I'm here for—I'm your ʻaumakua. She thought she heard a familiar teasing note in the *moʻo's* voice in her inner ear, and though she couldn't see him, she sensed Beosith tracking them into the shallower water.

They'd left the sharks behind at last.

Sam crawled across the netting and hugged her. "I'm glad the sharks didn't get you, sis."

Bea grinned, gave him a kiss on the forehead. "Me too." She looked up toward shore, her whole body shaking with the adrenaline aftermath. Somehow they'd made it into Molokai's wind shadow, and the Hobie was still headed generally toward shore and moving much slower.

"It seems like we can get there now. Why don't we paddle the rest of the way?" Nick handed Jaden Sam's abandoned oar as Sam unspooled the sail and let it inflate.

"Let the wind help us, too."

Bea moved to sit beside Sam as he controlled the sail while the boys used the oar and paddle. The wind still swiped at them in occasional gusts, and they'd plunge the paddles into the water to try to keep the cat pointed toward shore.

Sheer effort and a little wind power pushed them into a small, shallow bay, sand-bottomed and sheltered from the wind. Kiawe trees ringed the beach, and a red dirt road led up and away into the trees, toward civilization—or whatever was left of it.

22

SAM FINISHED PACKING UP HIS backpack in the cool of morning and realized he didn't have any shoes but the tabis. Soaked with seawater, they weren't the best to walk in. He took them off, inspecting his pruny feet and looking ahead at the road for kiawe thorns. The hardy scrub trees dropped brittle, thorn-covered twigs all around their radius—but the road, rutted and unpaved as it was, looked pretty clear. Up ahead, Jaden and Bea were already walking in the rubber slippers they must have remembered to pack, but Nick was still wearing his battered sneakers and jeans. He'd draped his shirt over a sunburned shoulder.

They'd rested in the shade of the trees all through the afternoon of that first day. They'd made a fire and roasted the fish, and Sam's belly was tight with all the fresh mahimahi he could eat. The aku they'd had raw, sliced thin with a little rock salt and limu from the rocks, mouthwateringly delicious, and a revelation to Nick. Sam thought it was especially tasty when eaten off the blade of his knife, which had mysteriously reappeared in his pocket. Mama had always forbidden him to use a knife to eat, but he was old enough to build and sail a boat, and he was old enough to eat off his knife without cutting himself.

They'd gone to sleep when the sun went down, worn out from the day and snuggled in their sleeping bags in the sand. Now Sam trudged barefoot, carrying his tabis, behind Bea, Nick, and Jaden down the rutted, red dirt road.

This remote fishing area was miles from Kaunakakai, the capital of Molokai, itself just a small town but several times the size of Lanai City. It was several miles farther still to their aunt and uncle's ranch in a verdant valley outside of town. Acres of kiawe trees and tall grass rustled around them in the morning light, seeming alive with whispers.

Sam pondered the miracle of Bea's rescue. There was something strange about how she'd been struggling to swim fast enough, and then it seemed like one of the sharks had risen from below and thrust her forward so she could grab the ring.

When he'd asked her about it, she'd said, "I was freaking out so bad, and there was so much going on in the water. I have no idea." Jaden and Nick had also been frowning, but it seemed there was no further explanation.

Sam had begun to work up a sweat, and his bad leg was aching, causing him to fall even farther behind, when they heard the muffled thunder of hooves. Sam hurried to catch up with the older kids, and they clustered together on the side of the road as a group on horseback rode up.

These were true Molokai *paniolo*—cowboys—wearing sweat-stained straw hats and seated on the kind of shiny-worn saddles that got that way from years of work. Four of them, intimidatingly large and adult, reined in their mounts. Sam spotted rifles in the saddle-tied holsters on their sides and pistols in their belts. Sam recognized one of them, Henry Kane, one of Buzz's fishing buddies and his cousin—and thus their family, too.

"Uncle Henry!" he yelled, dropping his pack.

"So what, boy!" Uncle Henry said. "What you doing? How you wen' get here?" Their voices fell into the rhythm of pidgin.

"We built one boat, we sail 'em from Lanai," Sam said proudly. "You know where Uncle and Aunty stay?"

"Where you think? They home. They going be so surprise fo' see you. Who dis?" He leaned forward on his saddle horn, indicating the others with a calloused brown hand.

"My sister, Bea. She always stay home with Aunty when we go fishing, and Nick. He and Jaden Apucan, they wen' help us get over here. Jaden come for news on what stay happening fo' take back to Lanai."

"We riding the roads—doing patrol. Good thing we find you kids first. Some mean kine people hiding out here. They'll take your stuff and beat you up for the hell of it." Uncle Henry leaned off his mount to shake hands with Jaden, Bea, and Nick. After introducing the other two patrolmen, he gestured.

"Climb up. We take you back into Kaunakakai." The kids mounted up behind the riders and they wheeled the horses to head back into town. "We hear folks on Maui having hard time," Uncle Henry said, as Sam leaned his cheek against the older man's worn chambray shirt and they rode down the dirt road. "People forget how for grow and catch their own food. But we never stop working the `aina over here."

"Same on Lanai," Sam said. "And my sister, she bring plenny seeds." Bea had packed one of those coffee cans to the brim with harvested seed, and it rode in her backpack now.

"The Kanekoas going be happy to see that," Uncle said.

Kaunakakai was a small town, though three times the size of Lanai City. The buildings of the town were done in false-fronted Western style, painted bright colors: pistachio green, robin's-egg blue, and brick red. Pickup trucks, the favored mode of transportation, lined parking stalls in front of the buildings—permanently parked, as it turned out.

All in all, Molokai people suspected they'd come through better than people on Maui or Oahu, according to Uncle Henry. No one knew if the solar event had reached as far as the Mainland, or what was happening there. The horses clopped down the asphalt road through town, and Sam felt like he was in a parade as children and dogs came running to greet them.

The patrol rode them right up to their aunt and uncle's house. The family's dogs, big black pit bulls named Tiny and Fuzzy, ran out on guard duty—but switched to slobbering and whining in greeting as Sam and Bea slid off the horses.

Jaden and Nick, looking nervous, took a little longer to come forward. By then, Aunty Hilary had run out of the house, yelling. "*Auwe!* What you kids doing here?"

She burst into tears as she clasped both of them in her capacious arms, weeping and kissing. It was all the welcome Sam had imagined and more.

Uncle Buzz came out, and their cousins, and it was a maelstrom of hugging and questions. Eventually they sorted out onto the wide, sheltering porch of the house. Bea handed the can of seeds over to her aunt, who was indeed very happy to have them, and Sam got yet another head rub from Uncle Buzz, his cousins plastered against either side. A little younger than Sam, they looked up to him.

"So. What gave you the idea to come here?" Uncle Buzz said, when the obligatory beer, snacks, and "talk story" had been dispensed to the patrol for their kindness in bringing the kids out to the house and the riders had got on the road back to town.

"Maybe I should answer that one," Bea said, to Sam's relief.

Bea relaxed as her aunt, clucking over the state of her hair, sat Bea between her knees on a lower step and pulled a brush through the long, tangled, salty tresses. "You can't even properly wash this hair until I get all these tangles out."

"Thank you, Aunty." This was just what Bea had been longing for when she pictured her aunt's face. It felt as good to be in the Kanekoas' house as she'd imagined, and she closed her eyes in bliss.

You're welcome, she thought she heard Beosith say.

"I asked you how and why you came here," Uncle Buzz rumbled. "And there's a reason for that." Uncle had his throw net out and was showing Nick how to repair a tear in the fishing line with a bamboo shuttle. Jaden was already at work sharpening hooks with a whetstone, and Sam was inside looking at comics with their younger cousins.

"I'm sorry, Uncle. I was the one who had the idea to come here," Bea said, her eyes tearing up a little as her aunt tugged at a knot in her hair. "We were staying in town with the Apucans after our house got taken over by a gang. After the disaster happened, I found Dad's truck, but he was missing. Then I just started thinking we needed to get to you, to be with our own family. Sorry, Jaden," she said to her friend, who had set down his work to sip on a glass of lemonade sweetened with honey like he'd never tasted it before.

Jaden flapped a hand. "I get it. No worries."

"You say your dad was missing?" Uncle Buzz's weather-beaten brows drew together over his broad nose. "Because he said you died."

"What? You've seen him?" Bea felt the blood drain out of her face. She was glad Sam was inside the house. Nick looked at her in concern.

"Yeah. He's here on Molokai. He took a boat out of the harbor, turned up in town in rough shape. He wasn't feeling well." Uncle harrumphed in his throat, a sound indicating his disapproval over Will Whitely's alcoholism, a widely known and little-discussed fact. "Anyway, he said you two were in the truck with him, in the accident, and that you'd died."

"What? That's a lie!" Bea could hardly form the words. Perhaps this had been a thought Beosith had planted in her dad's alcohol-soaked brain. *A thought that he'd chosen to believe because then he could abandon us.*

Her stomach went hollow with guilt—she was the one who'd called on the dragon to help them, and her father must have suffered so much, thinking they were dead! And yet, had he made any effort to find them? And she couldn't endure his treatment of Sam one more day. Even with all they'd been through, it was better than trying to manage Will Whitely, too.

Her aunt hugged her from behind. "That's why I was crying so much," her aunt said into Bea's hair. "I thought you were dead."

"Why would he say that?" Jaden's face was blank with incomprehension. "I don't understand."

"He must have hit his head or something," Bea said. "He's going to show up here to try to take us when he hears we made it over."

"Never. He's not taking you anywhere." Aunty Hilary resumed combing Bea's hair. "I wanted you to come live with us two years ago, when we could see he was getting worse after Angel passed."

The family sat in silence until Uncle Buzz said, "You have a home with us as long as you want one. Now, Jaden. We know you came to find out what's going on over here, and it's okay. In parts. We have the patrol keeping the peace, and people are taking care of their own—but the tourists aren't doing so well. They've got nothing we need but their money, and everyone's trading now, so the ones who work, who try to help—they're getting enough to eat. Speaking of." He gestured with his bamboo shuttle to Nick. "What you doing here with my niece and nephew?"

Bea saw Nick swallow and make some sort of decision. "I'm from Chicago area. I was in foster and I was on my way to live with my grandparents on Maui when our plane went down. I got separated from our group, who were spending the night in the Whitelys' house, when the gang took it over. I tried to rejoin the rest of the airplane survivors at the Lodge after traveling back to town with Bea, Sam, and Jaden, but there was a group running the Lodge that kicked me out. Said they had too many mouths to feed."

A short silence followed this. "You're going to hear that a lot," Uncle Buzz said. "But there's always food for someone who's not afraid to work."

"I'm not afraid to work," Nick said. "And I have some money." He reached to his waist and pulled off the salt-water-stained leather belt he wore. Bea felt her eyes widen as he opened a slit in the belt and pulled out a handful of cash, offering it to Uncle Buzz. "To pay for room and board."

"Your money's no good here," Uncle Buzz said. "But I'll remember you have some if we ever have need. No, it's working that will come in handy."

"I can work," Nick repeated, putting the money away.

"I can, too," Jaden chimed in.

Uncle Buzz was still focused on the Mainland boy. "So do you want to get to Maui? Find your grandparents?"

Nick's blue eyes were sad. "I know they didn't really want me. I came with Bea and Sam because I was learning how to survive on the ocean and land from them, and they were coming here. I don't have a lot of choices. But if you give me a chance, I'll work hard here."

Uncle Buzz smacked Nick's sunburned shoulder, making him wince. "Got a strong back, I see. We can always use that. We're putting all the land we can into garden."

"Let's get started with some baths," Aunty said. "You kids stinky, not to mention your clothes are filthy. I'll start heating the water." She got up and went into the kitchen, and the rest of them trooped after her.

Bea dropped her head onto her folded arms, content to rest on the front steps and savor the feeling of being home. And safe.

He's coming, the dragon said.

Bea lifted her head. Directly across the yard, petting the dogs' heads, was her father.

He was tall and ropy, with furrows of drink and sorrow etched deep in his cheeks. His profile was almost unfamiliar without the John Deere hat, and his blue eyes pierced her from wells of darkness. She looked wildly around, but everyone had followed her aunt into the house.

"Beatitude Whitely," her father said. "I thought you were dead."

Bea's father was here. *Here to take us away, here believing a lie.*

"What are you talking about? You must have hit your head." Bea stood up. Anger rose in her, white-hot and powerful. Anger she'd never been safe enough until now to show. Anger that was rocket fuel. "Maybe that's what you wished would happen, so you believed it."

He shook his head. "It doesn't matter now. Go get your brother. You're coming with me."

Their voices must have drawn the rest of the family, because Bea felt Uncle Buzz's hand descend to grip her shoulder, large and kind.

"We aren't coming, Dad. We're staying here with the Kanekoas. This is where we belong," Bea said, that anger strengthening her voice.

"You're *my* family!" Will Whitely's voice rose, as he pointed a trembling, knobby finger at her. "Shut your mouth, girl, or I'll shut it for you!"

Bea shook off her uncle's hand and strode down the steps to stand in front of her father.

"Take your best shot, Dad, but we're not going." She felt ten feet tall, her eyes on fire. He raised his arm, with that hard hand at the end of it, and Uncle Buzz's voice cut through the charged silence.

"Suggest you go now, Will. The girl said they're not going with you."

Bea shot a glance over her shoulder. Uncle, Aunty, their cousins, Nick, and Jaden all lined the porch and looked ready to pounce on her dad.

You don't have to live with him ever again, Beosith said. *If you don't want to.*

"Go, Dad." And she poked her father in the chest, just a small poke with her forefinger, almost affectionate. "Goodbye."

His arm never completed the backhand she saw in his weary, hard, sad eyes. The arm fell to his side, and he turned and walked away, his shoulders slumping. She watched him go and even felt a tiny bit sad for him—but when she turned and ran back onto the porch and into the arms of her family, she felt only happy relief.

Nick watched the tall, shambling man who was Sam and Bea's father disappear into the darkness. He could tell that man was the one who'd left the fading bruises on Sam, the man who'd kept them out at that house and stockpiled all the food and supplies and kept them away from the people of the town.

But because he was who he was, Bea and Sam had the survival skills they did. They'd at least had a father who cared about them in whatever way he could, while Nick's hadn't known he existed. He'd never been able to get his mother to tell him anything. "He was tall and handsome. An athlete, like you," she'd said. "But he wasn't ready to be a dad, and I didn't want him to know, and now I don't know how to find him. We don't need him, anyway."

But she'd died, and Nick had needed him. Someone. Anyone who wanted him, who gave him a place to belong. That's how Dodger and his crew had become his family.

Bea came to the door. "Come in. The bath is ready, and guests get to go first."

Guest. Not family. But he was glad to have that, at least, and a chance to go back on the straight and narrow from here on out. There was no need for pickpocketing or lies in this tough and honest island with these tough and honest people, and that at least was something—and so was the slender girl with the green eyes. He'd do a lot to be anywhere she was.

Nick followed Bea into the house.

Sam got into the metal tub after his sister, who'd had it after the older boys. Water was still an issue on this arid island. He was efficient, scrubbing briskly in the warmish, soapy bath, doing his hair, then getting into the cold-rinse tub whose water had been changed, washing the last of the grime of journey off him.

He was still rendered silent and in awe of his sister and her courage in confronting their dad. She'd poked the old man in the chest, told him to hit the road—and he'd gone, hopefully for a long time. Maybe even forever.

And as for him, Sam knew where his future lay now. On the sea, where his bad foot wasn't even an issue, and his uncle Buzz could teach him all he needed to know about being a fisherman.

23

BEA STOOD ON THE BEACH, looking at the loaded Hobie cat. The early-morning wind freshened across the Channel, and the new, real sail and metal lines hummed, rigged and ready to go. A real Hobie steerage system with double paddle-type rudders on a maneuverable tiller had been installed, pirated along with the rigging off a broken-down hull in the harbor.

The newly christened `*Aumakua* was almost ready for launch.

Jaden turned away from stowing items on the restrung trampoline. Two sturdy young men he was sailing with, who had family on Lanai and wanted to help out there, continued to prep the vessel. Both of them were experienced sailors who'd gone across the Channel, and as far as Maui, many times.

One of them broke out his ukulele for a departure mele. Family on the beach, gathered to see them off, sang along in Hawaiian. Bea stood with a hand on Uncle Buzz's old horse Lani, a plodding but reliable mare who had carried the two of them down to the little bay for the launch. Jaden had said his goodbyes to everyone else back at the house. Sam and Nick had stayed back to help on a new groundbreaking project on the land.

Bea felt a tightness in her chest as Jaden approached her, his brown eyes alight with the upcoming adventure and the sun sparkling on drops of water on the sharp line of his collarbone—a tiny detail she could bear looking at so much more than his eyes.

"Travel safe," Bea said. "No swimming with the sharks."

"Ha. I'll leave that to you." He stood in front of her, and she felt that something between them, something that made her heart thunder and the hair on her arms lift, as if a breeze passed over it.

"Can I kiss you?" he whispered.

She nodded, unable to speak, her eyes on his collarbone. He stepped closer and put his arms around her, and they fitted like they always had. She closed her eyes and tipped her face up, turning like a flower toward the sun—and the kiss was like a butterfly landing and staying a little while.

A hoot from the boat made them spring apart, and Bea felt a blush burn across her cheeks. "Come visit sometime."

"Soon as I can." They hugged one more time, fiercely, with all the strength in both their arms. Then he turned and ran back, and there was more hooting and laughing and three young men in surf trunks pushing the boat into the water. The sail snapped and belled open. They scrambled aboard into their positions.

Bea lifted a hand and held it there, a silent wave that Jaden echoed. She watched until the great blue ocean seemed to swallow the little craft in the flying spume of the Kalohi Channel and the beach had cleared of well-wishers.

Lanai's golden slope in the distance looked like a promise or a dream. The old mare bumped her with her padded velvet nose, and Bea sighed, leaned her head on the worn leather of the saddle, and contemplated if she needed to cry.

Why not? Nobody here but Lani and me.

"Beosith." She lifted her head to see the magnificent little dragon rise up out of the water, a good-sized white *kumu* flapping in his jaws. He shook the water off, much like a dog, and stretched out in the warm sand, holding the fish between his forepaws and crunching on his prize headfirst. Lani backed up, eyes rolling, and Bea moved her out of visual range and tied her to a bush.

"I haven't seen you much lately." She came back and sat beside Beosith on the now-deserted beach, resting elbows on her knees as she reached out to scratch his back. He fluttered those smooth, blue-purple scales, flicking the last of the salt water off onto her in a playful spray, and she laughed.

You haven't needed me much lately.

"I know. Things are pretty busy with the family." And indeed they had been. Working the garden, expanding the size to double, and helping Uncle Buzz refit his fishing boat to move under paddle and sail had been no easy task. Between major projects and the usual household chores, Bea hardly ever found herself alone. She thought of Nick, working hard to break ground with a pickax at home, and was glad he was still there.

She'd just kissed Jaden, but she still wasn't sure which boy she liked more. *Maybe it's okay to like them both?*

It's fine, right now.

Bea laughed. "I forgot you were listening to my thoughts. This isn't exactly a dragon problem I've got here."

I'm wondering if you need me anymore at all.

Beosith had found a small pond used for watering cattle near the Kanekoa house and had taken up residence there. Glimpses of him by a few *paniolos* and, of course, cattle who now refused to drink at the pond, had caused the legend of the *mo'o* to resurface. Bea had kept her mouth shut at several dinner-table conversations centering on the topic of powerful `aumakua,` and whether the *mo'o* were benign or evil.

It was beginning to become a problem.

I think I must go. I've been thinking so for a while. Besides, I've eaten everything in the pond. Even the toads. He rolled an eye at her, sending her a taste of how bad they were.

"Ugh. I'm sorry. But I don't want *you* to go, too." Bea threw her arms around his tensile, powerful neck, and he bent his head to whuffle in her ear, blowing curling hairs out of her braid.

I'll always come when you call.

And just like that, with one more fishy air kiss, he moved out of her arms and rolled in the warm, gritty sand, grunting with pleasure. He stood, shook himself, blinking his bright eyes, and then moved down into the ocean and, with a flick of his tail, was gone.

Bea lay facedown in the sand and cried.

She cried and cried some more. When she was done and had wiped the last drooly bits of sand off her face and climbed aboard Lani and headed for home, she realized something. For the first time since her mother died, the wall of tears inside her was gone.

Really gone.

She took a big deep breath, blew it back out on a giggle, and smiled.

"Thank you, Beosith."

You're welcome. He sounded as nearby as ever.

ACKNOWLEDGMENTS

Aloha, dear readers!

Special thanks goes to three wonderful schoolteachers who reviewed this manuscript for both content and readability, and gave a lot of helpful input! Mahalo nui loa to Don Williams, Bonnie Hodur, and Beckee Morrison. Each of you contributed something to make this a stronger tale. Thanks also to journalist extraordinaire Shannon Wianecki. Her article on mo'o dragons and 'aumakua in a Hawaii magazine publication was so excellent I asked her to consult on this manuscript, and now I'm proud to call her friend.

As a kid on Kaua'i, I grew up with parents who were aware and concerned about how dependent we are in Hawaii on imported food, fuel, and technology. My parents, worried about the gas crisis and shipping embargoes in the 1970s, stockpiled food and necessities against a "someday disaster." We ended up having to eat a *lot* of beans and rice because that disaster never came. Though times have changed in many ways, Hawaii's dependency on outside sources has not changed.

It was scary to me back then, and it still is now. Though that disaster hasn't happened it still could, and *Island Fire* is my exploration of a post-technology world in a place as isolated as any I could think of—tiny Lanai, right off the coast of my home island, Maui.

This first book is a test to see if anyone else is interested in this kind of story, this kind of "what if" world where all the things we know and depend on are taken away. If you liked *Island Fire*, please post a review and ask for more. *If you do, I'll write them!*

Much aloha,

Toby Neal

ABOUT THE AUTHOR

Toby Neal grew up on the island of Kaua`i in Hawaii. She has been a school counselor and therapist working primarily with kids and adolescents for the last 15 years, and says, "I'm endlessly fascinated with people's stories." Outside of work and writing, Toby volunteers in a nonprofit benefiting disadvantaged kids and enjoys life in Hawaii through beach walking, fishing, diving, bodyboarding, photography and hiking.

OTHER BOOKS BY TOBY NEAL

Middle Grade/Young Adult:
Island Fire
Wallflower Diaries: Case of the Missing Girl
Wallflower Diaries: Case of Dr. Feelgood
Wallflower Diaries: Case of the Mean Tree

Toby Neal also has a line of adult mysteries
and other stories set in Hawaii, below:

Lei Crime Series:
Blood Orchids (book 1)
Torch Ginger (book 2)
Black Jasmine (book 3)
Broken Ferns (book 4)
Twisted Vine (book 5)
Shattered Palms (book 6)
Dark Lava (book 7)
Fire Beach (book 8)
Rip Tides (book 9)

Companion Series:
Stolen in Paradise:
a Lei Crime Companion Novel (Marcella Scott)

Unsound:
a novel (Dr. Caprice Wilson)
Wired In:
(Wired series, Book 1, Sophie Ang)
Wired Hard:
(Wired series, Book 2, Sophie Ang)
Wired Rogue:
(Wired series, Book 3, Sophie Ang)

Contemporary Fiction/Romance:
Somewhere on Maui
an Accidental Matchmaker Novel
Somewhere on Kaua`i
an Accidental Matchmaker Novel

Nonfiction:
Under an Open Sky: Essays on Nature
(coming 2016)
Children of Paradise:
a Memoir of Growing Up in Hawaii
(coming 2016)

Sign up for Book Lovers Club or news of
upcoming books at http://www.tobyneal.net/

For more information, visit:
TobyNeal.net